# Merciless Heir – Billionaire Romance

## Rebecca Baker

# Chapter One

## KINGSTON

I'm willing to do anything to get what I want.

What's mine.

Including meeting some shady character to find my Sinclair jewel.

I push open the door to Fat Jim's. It's the kind of dive bar that should be filled with smoke and clandestine deals.

This place hasn't been discovered by New York's hipsters. It's real. Old school. Dark red and scarred tables and seats in the hole in the wall on the edge of the city in the Lower East Side.

And I'm hoping my quarry tonight will be what I need.

For the past month, I've had people out looking for the final Sinclair jewel. The coveted tiara, something steeped in whispered lore, is missing. Something I've known since after my baby brother, hound dog of the boroughs, fell from grace and smack bang into love's claw.

Love.

I don't give a flying fuck about love.

There was a time, once, I thought myself in love. But that was back in the day when I believed in dreams more than cold, hard money.

That woman ripped me off and I narrowly avoided a life of pain and payments, thanks to my father.

No one else knows of that shameful period.

Apart from me, that is.

I wear it deep inside as a constant reminder of openness. Of naïve ways. The stupidity of the heart.

But I'm not here for love, I'm not here for sentiment—at least not mine. I'm here for what belongs rightfully to me.

All I want is the final Sinclair jewel and it's gone.

There's a lot tied up in that damned tiara, rumored to be worth a fortune. Rumored to be worth more than its monetary value.

I know how my brothers see it. They see it as a symbol for something intangible. Some goddamn beacon to love. But they're happy. All three of them. All in love.

I don't see it that way, not at fucking all.

No, I see it how it is.

I see the story about it, the fact the Sinclair jewels represent something to others. I see how they've upped their value because they're old and bespoke and that makes them even more valuable on paper.

I want my hands on all of them. Though I don't know how, since my brothers gave their pieces to their ladies. Still…there are ways, and some of those ways are more above board than others I'm not about to sink to. There are loans and exhibitions. And bringing all the pieces together is something that pushes our family name in a way advertising couldn't do.

Yes, my Sinclair jewel is worth more. Just not the way the saps mean.

But it's gone and soon I'll be told that officially.

So, I've taken a sabbatical from my work to find it. Sabbatical for me, anyway.

I'm rich enough to step away whenever I feel like it. Although there is always more money to be made, so sabbatical from my real estate empire is more me stepping back and watching over others.

Some might say this is stupid, focusing on a trinket. And in a way it is.

I've got tangible things. Money. Power. An empire of my own. The only interest in Sinclair's—the family's very own empire that started our path to great wealth—I have is in what it can give me. The added shine, the deep roots some investors like.

But before I can have it among my arsenal, my trophies of wealth and power, I need to find the fucking thing.

So here I am in a dive, to meet someone I already don't respect—a notorious jewel thief. One revered and never caught, one who works, supposedly, on the right side of the law. One who is the darling of the rich and famous.

Midnight Raven. A stupid name.

This very well might be a bad decision.

I move across the scarred and uneven floor. The Sex Pistols play over the sound system, and the place is empty, save for a few people drinking with dedication or holed up in intense conversation.

The bartender, tattooed, wiry, and a man who's lived a colorful life from the lines and scars on his face, nods at me. I order bourbon—house—and take a seat at the bar, slapping down a fifty.

I'm dressed the part; old jeans and boots and a sweater beneath the black winter jacket that I now drape over the back of the stool.

My brothers would raise eyebrows if they could see me now, but they don't know everything about me. And I'm here on a mission.

It's not my birthday for a month, when winter sets in, and that's when my father's attorney, Jenson, is meant to deliver the posthumous quest from my father. Whatever that might be.

But with the tiara missing, and my search hitting dead ends, I'm upping the game. I've a feeling there's a barb in this road. Or perhaps it's the fact Jenson wants to speak to me tomorrow.

A gust of cold air sweeps in and I turn.

A woman stands there. Leather pants, a long black duster that swirls at her calves, and the kind of boots made for hard living on her feet.

She has short dark hair, hardcore asymmetrical pixie style. A shapely red mouth and eyes rimmed with black, slanting them slightly, like a cat.

She's beautiful.

And her gaze lands on me.

She holds it for a long beat and my blood thrums, then she slides it past me, and over the rest of the room.

Sadie Hess. It took me a long time to get a name, a photo. There's something vampiric about her lack of photos, even when she's been at events where every person and their purebred yapper is photographed. I wouldn't be surprised if she didn't show up in mirrors.

Sadie watches me without watching. I can feel her attention, like a caress. And I'd be lying if I didn't say it had a sexual pull.

She moves, stepping into the bar and crossing the floor. Sadie has a way of moving that's power and grace and lithe. And she slides in next to me.

"I'll have the same. On him." She points to my drink and waits until hers appears. She downs some and leans back, swinging to face me.

Her eyes are dark. In this light I can't tell the color, but I suspect somewhere between night sky and obsidian.

"That your normal way of practicing business?"

That red mouth curves up, but the eyes are cool and give nothing away. "Depends."

"On what?" I ask, a small thrill of something hot moving fast through my veins.

"If my boss is interested in taking on yours."

I give her the once over, which is easy to do. "Your boss? As in the notorious Midnight Raven himself?"

"Rumors and notoriety are interesting, aren't they, Mr. Sinclair?" Sadie finishes her drink and taps a short nail next to the glass as she puts it down. It takes about three seconds for the bartender to refill hers, and after another second, mine. The order isn't lost on me. "They build things up, and they get attention and can also hide truths. And, they can help get things done. Open doors. Do you need doors opened?"

"Depends on what's behind them." I shift a little closer to her. "And on whether you can deliver what I want."

"Depends on the reasons you're seeking help."

She taps in time to the drumbeat of "Liar", Johnny Rotten's iconic voice screaming the lyrics. Sadie's good. Not an incriminating word spoken, and I know she won't, but still I decide to test it. "What's the saying? To catch a thief you need a thief."

"I don't think that's a saying. And if it is…" She shrugs. "I can't help you."

"I'm not trying to trap you for the cops."

"Nothing to trap me for."

"So—"

"I know who you are." Sadie leans in close and I'm drawn by smoke and jasmine, just the merest hint, and a ghost of spice.

"You don't sound impressed."

"I'm not."

And she isn't. It's the truest thing about her that I've seen so far. A dislike shines stark from behind the smooth front of her. I'm not sure whether it's me or whether it's what I am, a billionaire, but while I find it intriguing, I don't really care. All I care about is getting what I want and from my research, Midnight Raven is the best.

"I can work with that. You have a name?" I let the question hang and take a swallow of the bourbon. It's not bad for a place like this. When Sadie doesn't respond, I do. I'm not backing down, but time is money and games here and now aren't my thing. And besides, I'm intrigued over whether she's going to lie. "Midnight Raven wasn't easy to get hold of—"

"Bullshit."

"—in regards to the right part of the operation. I don't need security or the glitter and sparkle of rubbing shoulders with an elite criminal. I need a job done. And for that, I need to know your name. Or I walk."

Her eyes glitter, and her mouth turns up, very slightly. "Sadie."

"Sadie." I say her name like I'm tasting it.

"But you knew that."

This time I only smile.

"Why did you pay for this meeting?"

"To fast track this. I'm trying to track a piece. The Sinclair tiara."

"It's missing?"

I raise a brow and she closes her hand around her glass, lifting it up. I do the same with mine. "Not going to ask if it's real?"

"You're a Sinclair. Why would you lie about the existence? Midnight Raven costs a pretty penny."

The muscle in my jaw works as I control the smile that wants freedom. "I'm aware of that. This meeting cost a fuck ton. But make no mistake, I paid because I wanted this to happen on my terms. And now. I'm not a fool, and I don't take parting with money lightly."

"Spoken like a true rich bastard." She stands.

For a moment, my heart picks up. She's fairly tall and lean, I'm a lot taller, but she has a way that commands. She finishes her drink and the bartender reappears and fills up her glass, then tops mine.

Sadie slips in close to me, between my thighs and my cock hardens, every nerve ending whispering touch. I don't.

"What have you got?"

Her soft words spoken against my ear send a bolt of electric heat through me and it takes a second to grasp she means the tiara.

"All I know is it's missing. I've hired others, but no one has anything. The tricky part is I'm waiting for the official word on this from my father's attorney."

"So, the attorney either has it or had it or knew where it was. Ask them. I'm not sure why you need Midnight Raven."

"Because I need the best. There'll be lies. My father is playing games from the afterlife." I'm pretty fucking sure it's tangled up somehow with my mother, and she's pulling all kind of strings, but I keep that to myself. "I need someone who has access to those who'd want such a piece and can get things done."

She doesn't answer, just gives me a look between cynicism and avarice, something that is more of a turn on than it ever should be. Then she leans in, her breath warm against my ear. "You want the impossible?"

"Midnight Raven thrives on the impossible."

"Rumors. Notoriety."

"The truth. I want the best. I want results. I want you."

We stare at each other as something loaded passes between us. "I'll take that on advisement," she says. And then Sadie Hess downs her drink and strides out of the bar.

I don't even realize I'm on my feet until I go to stand.

My head spins slowly.

I'm not sure if I like her.

But she's the hottest woman I've met in a long time.

And I pull on my coat and go to get my wallet to give the bartender a little extra in a tip.

I rarely carry much cash, just some for the bar tonight.

There's nothing in my pocket.
Or my other one.
Not even in my coat.
My wallet is gone.
No, not gone.
Stolen.
By Sadie fucking Hess.

# Chapter Two

## SADIE

L ifting Kinston Sinclair's wallet was stupid.

But fun.

He's a billionaire. He could destroy me a thousand times over. If he chooses to.

Still, it was definitely fun and he didn't notice.

Call it practice, making sure my skills are still honed. Or whatever you want.

I took it and he didn't notice. I half expected he would.

He comes across as that sort of man.

But he's clearly not.

I slide into the cold darkness, a street away, leaning back against the recessed building, my spot given extra shadow from the stoop and where a street light is out. I'm still, silent, and not one of the scant handful of passersby even flickers a look my way.

Satisfied I'm not noticed, I pull the wallet from my coat, the leather smooth and supple that comes from age and quality. I flip the black envelope open and go through the wallet's contents.

Part of me expected a gold or silver money clip. These days most people have all their payment systems on their phones, but it's nice to see a wallet that's not just for show. Something that's used.

Old fashioned? Or someone who's pragmatic and ready for all situations? I'm not sure, but I'd like to find out.

There's fifty dollars in two twenties and a ten, a shit load of cards including a black AmEx I itch to take, a driver's license proclaiming him to be Kingston Jeramiah Sinclair. It's his birthday in a month. Thirty-six. He's got blue eyes and black hair and he's six foot three.

The photo is of a serious man with great bones and features and doesn't do him justice.

In person, even in a dark dive, he's devastating. There's something hard and darkly dangerous about him that doesn't say real estate mogul or soft billionaire. And he's far too arresting to be anything as boring as handsome.

He's art.

Beyond that...?

Kingston Jeramiah Sinclair won't notice his wallet is gone and when he does, he'll call my number, which he thinks is an office, and he'll threaten and whine and shout.

It's what these rich fucks do.

He'll—

I stop. Something hot passes through me and I shiver. Awareness coils around me, holding me, drawing my attention back in the direction the bar lies.

A man. Tall. Lean. Eyes on me.

Kingston stands there on the empty, dark sidewalk, hands in his pocket, looking at me like I'm under a spotlight.

It makes me a little off-center, that. I can make myself seen, I can make myself invisible, and right now, I'm meant to be invisible. Yet he's seen me.

Slowly, deliberately he comes up to me and I drop my hand with his soft leather wallet to my side.

He stops, right there, inches from me, hedging me in.

"Sadie, I believe you left with something of mine."

Then he reaches out and trails his fingers along my left arm, down to my wrist and circles it, drawing my hand and his wallet up.

He plucks it free with his other hand and tucks it away, not bothering to open it. Not letting me go.

We look at each other and a shiver that has nothing to do with the cold goes through me.

No one is around, even though we're in New York at three-thirty in the morning. I'm still surprised he agreed to meet me at such a late hour. Not that I think his kind don't pull all nighters. But here? Where there's no glitter and comforts?

No.

But Kingston looks like he fits. And it isn't his outfit. It's him. Like he doesn't give a fuck for anything except what he wants.

And he's looking at me like what he wants is me.

My mouth turns dust dry for a second. What would his lips feel like? They look hard, but I've a feeling they can soften at the right moment. I've a feeling this man knows how to kiss, how to arouse.

"You're faster than most," I say with a cool touch in my words.

His thumb caresses that soft, sensitive spot on the inside of my wrist and his mouth turns in a cynical half smile, the shadows of the night broken by a car passing, and the beam of the headlights catch him, throwing his high cheekbones into a masterpiece of shadow and light. "Don't play games with me."

"How about we call it a test?"

"Or call you a common criminal."

Now I lift my head, letting it touch the brick behind me and look at him like I'm wanting something hidden inside.

It's probably backbone.

That sarcastic thought dies a quick death. He might be richer than half the born into it one percent, but he's got chromium in his bones. A ruthless edge I can taste on the air between us that goes beyond boardroom sandpits.

"There's nothing common about me."

Now he shows teeth. "Criminal?"

"That would be telling, wouldn't it?"

His scent is one of money, power, expensive leather-bound old books that hold secrets. A spice and musk with dark smoke and a hint of deceptive sweetness and it's a calling to the physical inside.

"You're Midnight Raven. There's no one else." He slides his other hand along my throat, resting his fingers against my jugular and the throb and beat of it echoes in my blood and ears.

I touch him, lay my hand on his chest. The heat of him beneath the open coat, the heat that radiates through the soft merino and silk sweater, belies hot, hard flesh and the air is alive with an intangible need that flares between us.

That need is want. Hot sex.

I ignore it, and will myself cool, my features a mask as I continue to watch Kingston.

"That isn't any kind of question, Mr. Sinclair."

"No, Ms. Hess. It isn't. And you are the coveted cat burglar."

"The media and the authorities handed out the name Midnight Raven, all because of a feather that ended up as a calling card. It's the smoke and mirrors of notoriety. Oz behind the screen." I smile and curl my fingers, deliberately moving down along his chest, stopping shy of his belt.

His poker face is almost perfect.

But that little sharp breath is physiological, something he can't help.

It feeds power in me.

Good to know the heat and awareness flows both ways.

I can use it if I need to. Manipulate it if I want.

"I use the reputation and the moniker Black Raven for my services. And people have put two and two together and come up with their own answers. I never correct anyone. And it serves me well."

He leans in, his mouth almost brushing mine, but he moves up to my ear. "So, you're telling me you're not that good?"

"I'm the best there is. As to whether I stole from those people...it's up to you."

"Thievery is still thievery."

"Sometimes it's art."

"And when is that?"

"When rich fucks like you are the object of victimless crimes. All the things taken were worth more via insurance claims. And every single person could buy those things or others like them ten times over and not scratch their bank accounts."

This is my fuck you speech.

It also happens to be true. When I did my work, back in the day—not nearly to the level of crimes that have been cast at my feet—I only took from those who could afford it. I never took pieces that I knew were loved for actual sentimentality.

This wasn't because I'm a saint. But because those pieces often weren't worth the price tag assigned to them, and when they were, they weren't worth the trouble. People came after those hardcore.

I was in it for the thrill once I had enough to live on. And I got out once I'd done enough. Transitioned, is the word. I transitioned from the dark to the shadows on the right side of the law and found I could make real money by tracking down stolen pieces and helping build bespoke security for clients.

"Us rich fucks," he says, voice devoid of rancor, "still don't like to be stolen from."

"Pity because you sure like taking from the great unwashed."

He laughs against my ear. "I don't care if you've stolen from the entire world or no one. If you're as good as people say, as good as my research tells me you are, then I want to hire you."

"To find a tiara?"

"The Sinclair tiara."

And fuck him, my fingers start to tingle at the thought of touching one of the infamous Sinclair jewels. These things have been shrouded in mystery so long and coveted by people that the chance to track down the shining star is almost too much to resist.

Not that I was ever planning on resisting.

"I can find it." If it's out there, even hidden in a secret room of treasures like some serious black market collectors have, I can do that. "I have connections. It's going to cost you a lot of money and it's going to take time."

He lifts his head, his fingers absently stroking my wrist and my throat and it makes me throb inside. I hook my finger into his belt. Hunger flares in his dark blue eyes that, even in the low light of the street, are utterly arresting with their striations of gold and copper.

"Something tells me you're going to have a month."

"And why's that?"

"Let's just say there will be strings. And those are things I'll deal with. Just the time frame is your problem."

I narrow my eyes as I slide my finger against the heat and strength of him. I'm low on his waist, not down enough to be indecent, but enough to tease him, see what he says, but he doesn't, just moves in, his body bumping mine.

A deliberate touch, and he's got an impressive semi there. I meet his gaze and his eyes are molten now, and they contain all levels of dare that shoot straight down to my clit.

"These things don't happen on your preordained schedule."

"Make them," he says softly. "And I'll pay you double."

"I haven't named my final price."

"I know. I'll pay. Half now, the rest when you're done."

His mouth is close, and I want it.

I don't think. Not beyond the erotic curiosity that's bubbling inside, not beyond the need that pushes.

So I don't think, I simply do. I close the gap and I brush his mouth with mine.

Kingston doesn't ask why. Doesn't do anything but wait.

And so, I do it again. Somehow it morphs. His mouth opens and mine does, too. And our tongues meet.

It's an explosion of pleasure and heat. Like the best parts of hell's inner chambers licking at me, urging me on.

His hand slides about my waist and he's hard now, the erection big and pressing into me and it makes the flames leap higher, makes bones melt and twist into pure pulsating need.

I wind my fingers in his hair and break the kiss.

This is stupid, this is courting trouble.

Then he kisses me.

And everything changes.

# Chapter Three

## KINGSTON

S adie kisses like a challenge. Like shock. Like an electric blast of erotic power that heads straight to my cock.

The kiss is unexpected and so fucking good I kiss her back because why the fuck not? I don't have to like the person I'm kissing. Just want to nail them and oh yeah, do I want that.

I drop my hand that still is light against her throat, the thrum of her pulse is out of control and beating hard on my fingertips like its own kind of dare or come on, and I rake those fingers down her side, under her coat to pull her even harder against me as I take control of this kiss.

She's hot and wet and soft. Her tongue knows how to dance. And she growls low, a sound that slides through me and makes me want to take her right here and now and fuck whoever sees.

I kiss her hard, an erotic exploration and then I change it to something softer and more devastating, even as she tries to up the ante of where we are.

It's cat and mouse. A game. And I'm not a fan of those...at least not normally. But this one. I can indulge.

I move from her waist, over the dip of her narrow lower back to her ass in the tight leather. Cupping her, I pull her hard against my erection even as I kiss her so slowly and light I'm driving myself crazy.

But I'm pushing her more. Right to an edge. And she grinds against me, her leather covered pussy against my denim covered cock.

There's something about that low rated simulation of sex that's so dirty it climbs down into my marrow.

And the kiss spins out into dark heat and the right kind of wetness, of tongues mating slowly, wanting more.

I let go of her and bring my hands up, deliberately brushing her nipples, making her hiss, driving myself a little madder, and then I take hold of her face, angling it so I can plunder.

It's opened mouthed, carnal, and so fucking hot I could burn into nothing. And her hands come up along my arms to my wrists, and then I break it. Finally.

Resting my forehead against hers, listening to the mingled music of our harsh and uneven breathing, I finally say, "That's not going to get you a discount."

"Asshole."

"You kissed me."

"Let's call it an experiment," she says, shaking me off and I take a step back, knowing I need to get things inside under control.

I nod, sweeping over her body, and her nipples show like hard little points against the tight black of her top.

We're standing in the shadows and if I hadn't somehow sensed her, that same awareness that spread through me when she stepped into the bar, I'd never have seen her. Would have walked right on by.

Her mouth is reddened from me and not lipstick as she lifts her chin, jamming her hands in the pockets of her duster. "You were quick."

"In realizing you took my wallet?" Somehow, I control the smile that wants freedom. I get the feeling giving her anything is a mistake. And I don't make mistakes with people.

Not anymore.

If there are mistakes and missteps to be made, they're to do with money, but those wild days are behind me, too. I use money to make money. Pure and simple. And if this doesn't pan out, paying her to find what's mine, that's one risk I'm willing to take.

"Because," I say, "if you're talking about anything else more...intimate, I assure you only when it's called for."

"I didn't ask."

"You didn't have to. Just like I'm not asking what that was about. Nothing more than a power play or a game. I don't like either, just so you know."

She raises one cool brow as those dark, fathomless eyes slide over me. "Call it curiosity. It won't be happening again."

We both know she's lying. But strangely, I don't want to kiss her again, as much as my body wants it. Those kisses riled and disturbed in ways I can't put into words. "We have a deal?"

"This is an interesting job. I'll let you know."

And she slips out from in front of me and walks away.

It's not until I'm in my car home that I check my watch.

It's gone.

I start laughing. For a yes she'll work with me, stealing my Breguet is up there in the fuck you department.

Closing my eyes, I settle back and wait for the car to take me home to Park Avenue.

I'm looking forward to round two.

"How's your new mansion in the sky, Kingston?"

Jenson's question is polite and not a hint of snark, but I give him the once over as I sit in his understated office.

"I live on the fifteenth floor of my newest acquisition. And it's beautiful. I'm almost positive you didn't summon me here to troll or to talk real estate."

I do dabble in different arenas; my company is powerful enough to fund projects, raze buildings, and do what I see fit to build money and power. But one of my sweet spots is old Manhattan buildings that I return to former glory with modern touches. Some I keep for high end, furnished rentals as there are a lot of people who want the ease of that as they flit coasts and continents; others I sell the apartments.

This building is beautiful and I got this, through some perhaps underhanded deals here and there, primarily for my use with the top floor and its roof garden. The irony of me living in what would have been servant quarters and now prime real estate is not lost on me. It's all leased out on the floors below, because money is money and I don't need an actual mansion of floors upon floors—mine takes up the whole of the building which spans half the block.

But as I said, I'm not here to discuss that.

I know why I'm here.

Jenson clears his throat and goes a little red, but before he can speak there's a knock on his office door and my mother comes in, somehow bringing freshness to the dark day outside with its cold and biting wind.

"Sorry I'm late," she says, blowing an air kiss my way.

I narrow my eyes.

"Time is money. Specifically my money, Mother."

"Kingston." A warning is buried in her voice, but I ignore it.

She's up to something, I know that.

The woman's prints are all over whatever this lesson she's hell-bent on handing out to her sons is, and now she has me in her sights.

Thing is, I'm just interested in the money, the worth of the jewel. Which is why I never said a word when Ryder told me about her message about it going missing.

One month today until my birthday. Seems I was right in my guess of where this might be headed. No quest written by my father before his death. But a quest is coming. With stipulations.

If she's got the fucking tiara and is pretending it's missing so I can jump through her hoops, we're going to be having a talk when this is all done. But until then, until I know more, I'm biding my time.

"It's a month early, but I'm pretty sure I know why I'm here."

Jenson makes himself busy by taking a seat behind his desk and going through a file that's on his desk, next to his computer.

"And why is that, darling?" Faye Sinclair is one of those timeless women who looks good no matter their age, and hers is well preserved.

I've no idea if she's had work beyond a filler or Botox or whatever the latest technique is these days, but if she has, it's a master class in subtlety.

"Why?" I sigh loudly, deliberately. "Because you're here and it's happy birthday dear Kingston in one month, that's why. I'm not in the habit of being called to see Father's attorney."

My mother seats herself in the chair next to me, crosses her ankles, and leans on the arm. Her eyes sparkle. "We'll cut to the chase."

Jenson clears his throat. "It seems, Kingston, your quest is missing."

"Along with the tiara." My mother sits back and shakes her head, but her gaze is on me.

If she wants to play games, then I'll play my own. I know my brothers and she'll know the message was passed on, but she won't know if I've done anything, so I just stay quiet. And wait.

"You're going to need to find it."

"Any...clues?" I ask.

"It was in a safe and when we went to get it as per the instructions it was empty."

I swing my gaze back to Jenson. "Maybe our father fell on hard times."

"Not at all."

I don't know if Jenson is using his lawyer face and tone or if he simply lacks humor. It's not like we're close.

"But if the quest isn't completed and the tiara back in the right hands, ours, then..."

"The company is lost," my mother says quietly.

I frown. "If someone apparently took the quest along with the final Sinclair jewel, then why would they keep it? I'm not sure my father's hand-written letter to me is worth money."

"You should respect your father."

"Should I, mother? It's not like he respected you."

She thins her lips. "I fight my own battles and you know nothing of our relationship."

It's interesting she says it that way, like they had one beyond whatever friendship came about after the cheating and their divorce and our father's penchant for younger models of Faye. But I keep that to myself.

"If you get the tiara," Jenson says, "by your birthday, then the company won't be dissolved."

"Dissolved?" My heart starts to beat hard and fast.

Mother nods. "Here." She opens her bag and pulls out a thick cream envelope. Her name on the front.

I take it as something flutters to the floor. Swiping it up, my mother plucks it from me before I can do more than briefly glance at the scrap of paper. I don't say anything, just open the envelope and smooth the letter out.

It's as she says. All his sons must be ready for their tasks, and the tiara is the crowning jewel. I wince at the pun. There's more. Our inheritance will be lost. It says if we take it and the jewels in question aren't in Jenson's hands when we're given the quest—ours to turn down or accept if we wish—then our inheritances are forfeit and the Sinclair flagship company will be dissolved.

I don't give a fuck about our inheritance. I don't think Ryder, Magnus, or Hudson does either. We're all billionaires in our own rights. We don't need that money. I'd like it, but I don't need it.

But the company dissolved? And the four of us siblings unable to buy it or even a share?

That's some real bullshit right there.

I'm looking for the fucking tiara, anyway, because I want it.

What I don't like is this twist. I don't like being screwed with from beyond the grave. I don't like whatever stakes my mother might have.

I don't like the added pressure of this shit that smacks of manipulation.

Rising, I pocket the letter. "I'll get that damn tiara."

And with that, I turn on my heel and stalk out the door.

No, I don't like that something which matters to us is on my shoulders, my responsibility.

But the thing I hate most of all?

What I saw on that paper.

One word.

Just one.

But I know what it means.

Raven.

Somehow, someway, Sadie is tangled with my mother.

I'll keep that to myself.

But I'm going to keep an eye on Sadie Hess.

Real close.

And I'm going to find out the truth.

# Chapter Four

## SADIE

I'm so bored I'm thinking of stealing something, just to keep my sanity.

Not even the hilarious light pop band pretending at jazz can rid me of the boredom. And the view from the eightieth floor of the modern and over priced sky mansion wore off after about thirty seconds.

It's been three days since I saw Kingston. There hasn't been more than an hour pass without memory of those kisses turning my stomach into a sudden rollercoaster of thrills.

Of all the stupid things I've done in a lifetime of stupid, that one might top them all. Because curiosity and giving into certain urges come with hefty price tags.

I'm not ever doing it again. Even if the thought of doing so burns a path of erotic need inside.

Christ, I think the band is jazzing up some old school Madonna. I wouldn't mind, but they truly suck. A rich person's idea of cutting edge.

These soirees are always boring, but this crowd of self-entitled mega rich get under my skin. I'm betting not one person here has held a real job, known what it's like to decide between food and rent—who am I kidding? Make that Balenciaga and opera tickets.

I'm here doing a job the run of the mill security services out there could have done. They live among the clouds with a bird's eye view of the park and Manhattan, Brooklyn, Queens, and the rest from the other windows in this tower with a doorman who trained at Fort Knox protection detail. So slap some state-of-the-art security on the triplex, hone their insurance, and call it a day.

Instead, they want a gossip piece, they want the Raven. They want me. They want the glamor of notoriety. Of picking over whether I'm the real deal, work for the real deal, or just someone who slapped a similar name on a shingle and dropped a few pointed hints and things anyone who followed it all would know.

It doesn't matter to them. The risqué gleam of the idea does.

I fucking hate my life.

Still, it makes me more money when I did steal and in places like this, someone with skill would be robbing them blind of the best pieces and they wouldn't know.

I make small talk but mostly keep to myself.

Kingston's watch flitters across my mind. It's real, of course it is. And it's stunning. Worth a few million, not one of the top of the line Breguets, but I like it more than some of the ones with the double digit million dollar tags.

"Sally." Jemima Mao comes up and holds two coupe champagne glasses filled with the odious bubbles, and she presses one in my hand. I take it. "What are your thoughts?"

"On the party? Security or the view?"

"Oh." The petite dark-haired beauty waves a hand. "Security."

"I have some thoughts."

Her eyes go round and I point out things anyone can, like a new system that upgrades easily some different excellent private response teams in the area. And how insurance is of the utmost importance.

I feel like a vacuum salesperson.

"Did you—"

"I work for Black Raven, that's all." I smile as I say this.

The words flow easily. Lies and untruths have always come naturally. I suppose having the blood of a con artist in my veins gave me something. And this tale is one I've stuck to, kept bare bones so no one can ever compare notes and come up with anything like the wrong kind of inconsistency.

I'm good enough not to be verbatim every time, because that smacks of rehearsal and lies, but I keep it the same in sentiment and meaning and close enough in words.

Not that these people would care. They'd love it and my income would rise exponentially, but I do all right and greed is a downfall waiting to happen. It's why I got out when I did.

I let them weave their rumors, and build on them. I let them gossip and wonder. It all works to my advantage. I'm also exceptionally good at what I do and what I did.

Her face falls a little and she says, "So there's nothing special to do?"

"No one's about to scale the outside of the building." But I give her what she wants. That sense of special. "But with you, yes, there's a lot to do. You have unique taste and I can think of a number of ways someone can come in and take things tonight. I can see how people could get in here even with the best of the best. But I see you see that."

"Oh," she says, sipping deep from her coupe glass, "I do."

It makes one of us, but this is part of my job, so I weave the spell. Walk the fine line between thrilling her and pleasing her. They're so close, those things. Too much one way and she won't spend big. Too much the other and she'll turn paranoid.

Truth is nothing is foolproof. And most of the time it's fine. She wants to feel special, part of the elite in taste and money.

"I'll finish up observing, testing for weak pockets, and we'll set up a time in the next few days to really go over everything."

"Not tonight?"

This party will continue long after I make my way out. But I just say, "We'll touch base."

"These glasses, did you know the coupe was modeled on Marie Antoinette's breasts?"

I just smile. It's one of those enduring tales that aren't true, but I keep it to myself. "These glasses are mid-Nineteenth Century, French, aren't they?"

Her hand flutters and her eyes go big. "Yes!" She sidles closer. "Do...you know him or her?"

I always get asked that and I do what I always do, give that knowing smile. "I'll never tell."

It's enough to get them recommending me to others. And an embellished story to lunch over as the star for the next month.

Yeah, I hate my life.

I get out of the conversation and move about the great room that's combined with a formal living room. It's vast, half the apartment and then I wander off, taking my time, so I can explore the rest.

Everything is white and chrome and boring art. The kitchen is pristine and overlooks a giant breakfast nook and the most formal looking, *Fine Living* magazine ready, informal family dining table I've seen.

Every appliance is state-of-the art in the kitchen, and I doubt it's been touched except for photo shoots. I keep going, past the giant formal dining table that is a stand out piece of wood and chrome, marred by the overuse of crystal vases and art pieces; down the hall and into the second kitchen.

This is full of activity and action. The waitstaff from the high-end caterers are buzzing and loading trays and I move past, through another set of doors to explore the place properly.

It's a perk of my job. I don't need to do this at all, I can see what they need from stepping off the lift and to the front door. But I like to explore, learn the layout.

Old habits, it seems, really do die hard.

I explore the entire triplex, full of the kind of art only a fool would steal. It's expensive, but it isn't worth anything more than ticket price. And the jewelry is pretty and expensive but nothing stands out. Those pieces which she'll have will be in a safe. I don't bother looking for those.

I finally finish, having killed an hour if not the champagne. I make my way back into the great room where the band is playing jazzed up Celine Dion.

Settling in against the wall I observe the rich overindulging and being gauche.

My mind returns to Kingston. I'm going to have to return the watch. And I'm going to need to stop fucking with him and say I'll take the case.

I'm already working it. I have feelers out. I'm researching. I just... I just don't want to see him again.

Or maybe it's that I do. Too much.

I don't like him, but he calls to me. It's physical. A throbbing, thrumming ache and right then, I could almost swear he's there, I've been thinking about him so much.

That darkly spiced, slightly sweet, expensive scent pervades. And my breath catches in my throat as I start to tingle with heightened awareness.

And just as I turn around and meet his gaze, he speaks.

"I want my watch back."

# Chapter Five

## KINGSTON

She's even more beautiful than last time. That hardcore pixie cut is smooth and sleek and sophisticated. Her mouth a muter red. Eyes softer with the make-up and the dress fits her slender and sleek curves with a black shimmer.

The heels and black stockings with the seams finish the look.

She's a million miles away from the woman I met three nights ago.

I prefer the other one.

Sadie's a woman who should command attention, but she's very good at slipping it when she wants, like now.

Her eyes narrow. "Following me?"

"My watch."

"Maybe you misplaced it," she says, looking at me from lowered lids, the sweep of long, curved lashes unexpectedly sexy as she does so.

I take a glass of champagne from a passing waiter and wish to heaven it was something stronger, something less bubbly and frou-frou. It's not my drink, but the upside is it's easy to nurse. "Do I look like that sort of man?"

"I don't know."

"Or just a man you try and jump?"

"That was nothing more than an experiment, one I'm not about to repeat."

"Good. When you kiss me, you need to mean it, not be playing games."

Her mouth curves. "That kind of thing is nothing but games."

"Sex?"

"And all it comes with. All the things people attach to it."

Those words slide about me and it's like she's a unicorn, a mythical woman after my own lust-driven heart. Most women will say they don't want more than sex or the right kind of relationship where things are on the table and in the open, along with the exit point. But then something happens. Either they're lying or they develop feelings.

I get out before that shit ever happens to me. Once was more than enough.

But Sadie, she isn't looking for anything either. She doesn't like me. I'm not sure why, apart from I'm loaded. I don't like her kind, but her…she's hot and soft and she can kiss and the fire that burns hot between us is there whether we want it or not.

A fire I've no intentions of dabbling with again.

I won't lie that it's fun pushing her, watching for cracks. Like when she first saw me, the leap of light and smolder in her eyes before she dragged it back in.

"Interesting theory," I say, circling close to her, breathing her smoke and jasmine scent in, just as my gaze drops to linger on her exposed clavicle. The line and shadow of the delicate bone beneath her skin is accentuated by two small freckles.

She takes a breath, drawing my gaze to her breasts that are draped in the delicate material that shimmers darkly. It shows her curves, but there's a demureness about the cut, the neckline that dips to hint at what lies beneath—not put it out on show. It's hotter than it had any right to be. Just like her.

"Yes," she says, the dryness like centuries old dust, "because you're waiting for true love to drop in on you."

"I don't believe in love."

"Neither do I. It's a construct developed by the patriarchy to keep women in check."

I smile, and close the gap between us, letting my fingers trail against the soft smoothness of her shining hair. "I think we know it's the other way around."

"Only because women have been taught their shelf life is short."

"So, a true romantic, then?"

Her smile flashes like a knife. "Just like you."

"We should run away."

"Misery does love company."

I laugh. "You keep that up, Sadie, and I'll start liking you."

"Call me Sally in here." Her voice is barely audible, yet it shimmies through me. "And we can't have that happening."

"Give me my watch and when are you starting work for me?"

Her hand slips along the side of my suit and I'm overcome by the urge to check to see if she stole anything. Except I don't have anything in that pocket. Sadie's expression says she knows exactly what I wanted to do.

So I don't.

The music in this hellhole is terrible. The place filled with the kind of interior decorating that's insanely expensive, generic, and lacking in individual taste. Like a show apartment. And I'm betting someone like Sadie Hess hates it as much as me.

"I never said I would work for you."

"You will," I say. "You can't resist the challenge or the money." I look her over. "I'm betting it's the thrill of the challenge over the money that will hook you."

"It'll be the money, too. So, are you stalking me?"

"What would you do if I said yes?" I'm genuinely curious. We both know it's not stalking, but I did make it my business to find out where she'd be.

"I'd say I'm not interested in you."

"We know that's a lie."

"I don't like you, Mr. Sinclair."

I smile. "And I don't like you. Like has nothing to do with interest."

"Anything we do will be strictly business."

I take a sip of the warming champagne. "Like stealing my watch was business?"

"Maybe you lost it."

"No. I didn't lose it or misplace it. You took it."

Sadie smiles.

"You're also working for me."

"And," she says, "like I keep saying, I'll let you know."

"And when will that be?" I don't bother keeping the hard edge from my voice. All that gets is the merest flicker of a gaze from her.

"I'll let you know when I know."

"You have two hours. Then I'll go with someone else."

There are others. They just don't happen to be as good as she's meant to be. As Black Raven or Midnight Raven or whatever she wishes to call herself.

I can make do. Top notch jewelers and PIs exist. People with niche skills that I can use. They all exist. I have a list. And not one will cost what she does. Not one will give me the headache she will and yet...

I want her.

Maybe I'm no different to the rest of the society. Maybe it's the thrill of using the services of someone who used to steal from the rich. Maybe it's the fact she's no Robin Hood and she harbors a hard-edged dislike of my kind.

Or maybe it's her.

She mutters something under her breath, creatively crude. And I glance over to see Jemima Mao making her way to us. My gaze meets Sadie's and her mask slips, the dislike is palpable, and I can taste it, but then she's cool and accommodating and smiles.

I almost point out Jemima married up, monetarily. Her husband's the one born into wealth and power and is figurehead of the tech company his father created. I use the term tech company loosely. His father created a new computer chip back in the day and that's what they do. Create and make hardware and Mao himself sits as CEO and lets others do the work.

Jemima, on the other hand, is a lawyer. One who came up from nothing and carefully created her own image while riding the Harvard HLS Grant program. She graduated top of her class and is the kind of lawyer anyone smart wants to handle suits that come their way.

I know, because I've hired her.

She doesn't have a practice anymore, per se. Just does jobs she wants. So, she hides the shark beneath the layers of bubbles her husband likes, and, I suspect, she enjoys. The idle rich woman she is here is worlds from what she is when she dons her law persona.

Thinking about it, maybe Sadie has a point about what women do for love. This is what her billionaire husband wants and this is what he gets. And she gets...all this...

"Kingston," she says as she comes to a stop. "I see you've met my guest of honor, Sally."

"I have."

Her gaze sweeps me and then Sadie. "You never come to these things." Now Sadie's gaze is on me, assessing. "I hope you're not trying to steal my star attraction."

"Not until she's done here." I sweep my hand through the air. "I just decided to drop by after one too many meetings today."

I might be on sabbatical, but there are some things I can't and don't want to get out of. Like the meetings today. Like nailing Sadie down. In a non-sexual way, of course.

"You know how it is, one too many meetings and a soiree is just the thing," I add.

She laughs like I said something hilarious and Sadie's expression doesn't change, but there's that same dislike that beats in the air. "I know you're going to want to hire Black Raven for your new place."

The elevator dings and she breezes past.

"Y'know, Sally," I say before I can stop myself, "don't underestimate Jemima."

"These people. Of course you defend them. You're all the same."

"Really?"

"They gush like I'm a circus attraction."

"You make yourself that to them and you know it," I say, shifting to face her. "What? Did you grow up poor after some rich fuck stole your daddy's money?"

"That's what your kind do. Get richer by screwing the system and charging the little guy more and more and more."

I just laugh. "You screw the system by stealing from us and turning that to your advantage. I don't think we're that different."

Her eyes are pure, burning hostility. "Galaxies apart, Kingston." She pauses. "What did you mean about our host?"

"Your employer?"

"Client." She waits.

"Jemima comes across as a ditz whose biggest thrill in her life is you and yeah, she'll lunch on stories of your being here, doing her security system, but I've seen her slice apart powerful men with one word. She's a kickass, killer of a lawyer."

"But Mr. Mao likes ditz."

"Mao's an idiot whose wealth rivals mine. Jemima made adjustments to get the life she wanted."

"You all disgust me."

I smile because damn if I don't like her. No, I don't, not really. "You talk like you have morals. You don't. You'd rob everyone blind in here if it suited you."

"And you have morals?"

"I'm talking about you. And there are all kinds of morals, *Sally*."

"Like shades of black and white? You'll twist anything to suit yourself."

"And so will you."

Jemima walks past, and flashes an enquiring look at Sadie.

She sighs. "Duty calls."

"I expect an answer in less than two hours. Or I'll get someone else."

She doesn't answer. Just walks off.

I set down the glass on a tray held by a passing waiter and go to the elevator and hit the button.

Stepping in the empty space in chrome and white, I go down a few floors and then transfer to the equally empty one for the rest of the building and take that to the foyer. I could have taken the public one all the way, but that meant picking my way back through people who just might want to talk to me. So I took the private one.

Outside, I lean against my car that found a spot outside. It's cold, but I don't bother getting my coat from my driver. Right now, with the dark ink sky above, the lights of Manhattan giving the place a softer glow, I like the bite of the cold. It keeps me sharp.

I gambled in there. Giving Sadie an ultimatum of two hours or I get someone else is a risk because something tells me she doesn't like ultimatums. And if I fail, I'll do that; get someone else.

But I don't think I will.

For one thing, someone like Sadie would kill to get their hands on a Sinclair jewel. So would most people, but for a cat burglar of her caliber, it's a coup to be the one to find it. If it was stolen, steal it back. To touch, look, evaluate. All a privilege.

For another, I saw that scrap of paper my mother dropped.

Sadie's going to take the job.

She's just fucking with me.

But I've had enough of that. I need to move.

Sadie will come down. Sooner rather than later.

Funny thing is, I hate those people, too. And I'm more than aware I could have been one, so could have my brothers. Instead, we all chose to work. With a push from Father. And we worked hard.

I'd never say we had it hard, like many out there. And we did come from a place of privilege, but we earned what we got. We built our businesses and companies ground up.

Those people…so many just took what they were given and did nothing with it, other than be seen at the right places and donate to the best causes and call it a tax write off.

Even Jemima. She traded in her career for luxurious boredom, the kind of cage she perhaps enjoys, but is still a cage. She could have had it all.

Then again, maybe she didn't want it all. Maybe what she does now and who she is, is where she wants to be. We don't socialize. And I honestly don't care enough to find out.

And Sadie? I know a little about her, but most of her past is hidden away. Fine by me. I want her to get me my dues, not hand me her life story wrapped in a bow. But I'll be keeping an eye on her, that's for sure. We're a little too alike. And not just in our dislike for those who like to be idle, rest on haunches not of their own making, and rub unearned glory over themselves like some kind of tanning lotion. No, we both have a ruthless streak. And I don't trust her not to try and rob me blind if she could.

She can't, though. I'm not a pushover and I'm a different breed from those above.

A woman steps out of the glass and steel foyer, heels eating up the pavement as the cream coat on her lays open and shows me flashes of shimmering curves in black. And her gaze zeroes in on me as she continues, right on up to where I am by the curb.

I want her mouth again.

Just to see if it tastes as good as I remember.

I don't make a move.

"If I'd known I'd inspire this kind of devotion in you, I'd have gotten you a signed photo."

"Well?" I ask.

She sighs. "I was working. It's what I do."

"Yes, I'm aware of the concept of work, Sadie."

"Don't look at me like I'm a criminal," she says, stopping short of me a few inches. "I'm overhauling her security."

"And casing the joint?"

A small smile touches her mouth. "I do that for fun. Not work."

It would be part of the job, though. I can see that. And my needling her isn't as satisfying as I want it to be. She's too good at keeping most of her responses under lock and key.

"The clock's ticking, Sadie. What's your answer?"

"I still have forty minutes."

"I'm changing the rules."

"Your type always does. And I'm thinking. Still."

She turns to walk away, something I'm beginning to think is a signature move on her part, and it probably is. So I wait until she's taken four or five steps. Then I speak.

"One last thing, Sadie."

She stops, like there's something in my tone. And there is. Slowly she turns, tilting her head to one side.

That scrap of paper.

It's no coincidence.

"What are you up to with my mother?"

# Chapter Six

## SADIE

M y skin prickles and even though it's cold, a bead of sweat threatens to trickle down my backbone.

"Your mother? I don't swing that way."

"Neither does she." The cool amusement on Kingston Sinclair's face belies the steel and displeasure beneath the words. "You're avoiding my question. Think very carefully before you respond."

"Or?"

"I'll get someone else."

He folds his arms and the figure he cuts in the suit is utterly mesmerizing. He makes it hard to draw an even breath. Kingston is equally at home in suit and in jeans and that pure female part of me is there for it.

What the hell is he like without clothes?

Impressive, I bet.

When we kissed, I touched him, ran my hand down his chest, over hard delineated abs, and...and even though the soft merino wool sweater he was hot, hard, and I swear not even an inch of fat.

What the fuck am I even thinking?

I don't like him or anyone of his kind.

"You can…" I trail off. Turning him down, pushing him to hire someone else isn't part of the job description.

I'm having fun, yes, by toying with him and I'm not meant to start until I got the green light, but going a step too far will screw everything up and I'm not into losing money.

"Can what?" he asks me, voice soft, that steel cold and hard at the center. "Because I don't like being fucked about, Sadie. And there are others."

"I'm the best."

"Most notorious," he says, countering. "And notoriety isn't important."

He's playing me right back. Kingston Sinclair isn't a man to put up with games unless he wants something. But everyone has a limit. So I pick my words carefully, because I'm in trouble if he goes with someone else.

"But my skills are."

"Again, there are others. So. My question."

About his mother. I use my carefully handpicked words. "I don't know her."

I don't know Faye Sinclair. I've met her, talked with her, agreed to a job she's paying me for, but having him pay me too, getting paid double for the same thing, is so delicious, so delightful I'm in love with the idea. But know her? No. I don't know her. So I'm not lying.

Kingston isn't a man to underestimate. Those striking dark blue eyes with the hints of coppery-gold spark fire, and a low smile curves his hard mouth that can kiss so sweet, like he knows I'm working a loophole.

He probably does. He's exceedingly smart.

Kingston straightens and opens the door to his car, and gestures in.

"A strange man picking me up on the street? What's next? Candy?"

He laughs suddenly. "You like candy."

"Everyone likes candy."

"Talk to my brother, Mag about that one," he mutters. He lifts his gaze past me to the sleek, modern apartment scraper behind me. "You coming? Or you hoping to sign autographs?"

"You're an ass."

"Probably, and I'm not a strange man. We've kissed."

"That doesn't stop you being strange," I say, looking from the inviting comfort of the back seat of the car, and to him. "And that's not happening again."

"I didn't say it was. We're not done, Sadie. Get the fuck in."

Behind me, voices rise and I narrow my eyes at him but slide past him and into the car. He follows.

Through the tinted windows, the darkness of the park with its golden muted lights moves past, and I'm way too aware of the man next to me. He takes up too much space. He makes me too aware of him, of every shift and breath and that dark, expensive leather and spice of him with its undercurrent of smoky sweetness winds around me.

I pick at the material of my dress on my thigh.

"Nervous?"

I stop. "Should I be?"

"I don't know. Depends on what you're up to here."

"Where are we going?"

He's looking at me. I can feel the burn of his gaze and I shiver. "I get why you don't like those people, and I don't give a shit if you like me or not—"

"I don't."

"But what I don't get is your playing with this offer. Perhaps you think I'm not a man of my word. That's a mistake, because I am and if I say I'll walk, I will. There's only so far my amusement at your little game will get you."

"Maybe I want to see the kind of man I might be working with."

He sighs and we head to the Brooklyn Bridge. "Your beloved morals again."

"Let me guess, Brooklyn Heights."

"I can take you to Canarsie if you'd like."

"The less time in this car with you the better."

"Your winning personality led you into a life of crime, I see."

I look at him. "Meaning?"

"There's no way a little Grinch like you could hold a real job."

And I start laughing, so hard I think I'm going to cry black tears of mascara. This man is unexpected. "You've discovered my dark secret. Yours?"

"Me? I had to become a billionaire real estate mogul because eating baby souls is expensive."

"Brooklyn Heights it is." I close my eyes and settle back, not saying anything more until we pull up, because if I don't watch myself, I just might start liking him.

Brooklyn Heights is the most affluent in Brooklyn. The beautiful buildings and tree lined streets are dotted with upscale bars and restaurants, along with the neighborhood haunts. It lacks the pomp of the well-heeled of Manhattan.

Kingston leads me to a basement bar on the corner of Love Lane and Henry Street.

This is anything but a dive. It's intimate, expensive, and one of those places that get popular via word of mouth.

Kingston leans back as cool jazz weaves through the place, there to lift the ambience. This is the real deal, no BTS dressed in jazz sounds.

"I'd think," he says, strong fingers curling around the low ball glass of Japanese whiskey—I can't remember which one he ordered, only it's expensive, because of course it is—as he studies me, "that you would snap up this job without the games."

"And why would you think that?" I pick at one of the olives on the little plate between us, my Empress gin cocktail sitting untouched next to me.

He smiles and takes a sip. "Jewels. A rare piece that carries a story with it."

"A rumored piece," I say. He knows he's got me. Smug bastard. "It might not be worth a thing."

"But you want to find it, don't you? And, you want to find that out yourself."

And damn it, he's right. I do.

A Sinclair jewel? Something that until recently hasn't been seen? The whispers in the different worlds I've moved through are the final piece, the tiara, is meant to be the best, and worth the most if one was to split them up.

The whispers also talk of if the Sinclair jewels did still exist, then they were so elusive they might well be ghosts.

I doubt Kingston knows, but there have been attempts to break into different Sinclair enclaves to find them. Nothing came of it. Anything Sinclair I steered clear of, because their reach has always been vast, and retribution not worth it.

So, to take this route, to work with a Sinclair—or two of them in this case, even if the man with me doesn't know that—and have a chance to get my hands on the tiara?

It's too delicious, too tempting, to resist.

I want my hands on it.

I want to see all the Sinclair jewels up close.

Maybe get my hands on one for myself.

I know I could, if I do it right, have one replicated and replaced.

I'm thinking that should be the tiara.

The price that thing will fetch...I breathe out. That price is worth the entire sky.

Kingston leans forward. "From that look on your face, you're planning on a lot more than a simple yes to working with me."

"What look?"

"The one you had right before you slipped your cooler than silk expression back in place, Sadie." He slides a finger along the condensation of my glass, his flesh so close to mine it makes my breath stutter in my throat. "Been out of the game a little too long?"

I meet his gaze. "You're seeing things that aren't there."

"No," he says, "I'm not. And you'd be wise not to plan anything other than the help I'm going to be paying you for. Got that?"

"Like it's the clearest glass."

"Good." He drops his hand, fingers skimming mine, sending a delicate thread of electricity through me. Then he leans back in his chair. "What drew you to this life?"

"The paid vacations and healthcare."

He laughs and shakes his head. "You should watch yourself there, Sadie, or I might start liking you."

"We can't have that."

The laughter dies. "No, we can't."

I take in a shaking breath and follow it with a deep swallow of my herb and floral drink that's like a spring morning in the countryside. Or what I imagine one would be like. I'm not really one for the countryside. "How do you know this place?"

"Montague's?" Kingston looks about at the mix of people in there, some sharing bites and some small meals. Rich people, the well-to-do, all glossy and confident and having a quietly good time.

But it's not like Billionaire's Row or the Upper East and West sides, or, god forbid, Park Avenue. These people are a mix of various tiers. Various dress. There's a realness here I somehow prefer and I look back at Kingston, who's now looking at me.

"This isn't the kind of place that's in Time Out New York."

He smiles lazily. "You're thinking of my youngest brother. I don't give a fuck about on trend or old school places for the rich and bored."

"You like this?"

"I hope so. I own Monty's. And half the block."

"Of course you do." A man of many hats, one who can spin different and varied pies all at once, and spin them right into pie stores that rake in money.

"At least my earnings are above board."

"At least I don't crush the little person to get ahead."

"You like fighting. I should warn you, the particular brand you practice might get you unexpected results."

I take another sip. "Like what?"

"Turning me on." Kingston doesn't smile as he says this.

And I shiver.

"The clock," he says, "has stopped ticking on your time. I'm going to need an answer as I've already given you past the two hours, Sadie. Let me know, or I walk and your chance is gone forever. What's it going to be? Yes or no?"

# Chapter Seven

## KINGSTON

*Yes, I'll do it.*

That's what Sadie Hess said the night before.

Followed by, *I'll start and be in touch.*

I lay in bed, one arm thrown over my face. It's five a.m. and I need to get up and work out. I need to do a lot of things before I hit my own trail on things.

She stretched her game and my patience almost to a surgical breaking point, and then she told me what I knew she'd say all along.

One more minute and I'd have walked, no matter what she said.

She's a pain in the ass and dangerous. I'm not yet sure in what way she's the latter, but she is.

Sadie's also lying about my mother.

I'll take her answer for now. She sidestepped with a very logical answer, but it wasn't what I was asking and we both know it. My mother is up to something and Sadie plays things so close that pushing isn't going to get me anywhere. At least not yet.

And regardless, me seeing that scrap of paper isn't the point. I sought Sadie out. I want the best and I'll use the best.

I'm just going to need to keep a close eye on her, that's all.

Dropping my arm, I get up and head to my gym.

Magnus is saying something and I'm not listening. It's not my brothers bore me; we're close and they're more than family—they're friends, something I don't have among people on our tier.

Mainly because I'm in agreement with Sadie there.

I don't like the mega rich.

Ironic, I know.

Something hits me and I snatch the wad of paper before it hits my lap. Over the low hum of the exclusive club we're having lunch and drinks in, I say, "Was that needed, Ry?"

My brother shrugs and leans back in his chair, sticking his hands behind his head and giving me his shit eating grin. "You tell us. You're somewhere else today."

"Sorry." I run a hand over my face and turn my phone over so I can't see the screen. "Thinking about the latest."

"From beyond the grave?" Hud pushes his plate away and toys with the cloth serviette.

Magnus raises a brow, not looking the slightest annoyed I'd tuned out. "Or from across the divorce table."

We're in agreement on that. Our mother has her elegant fingers all over this. "Yeah. Seems that if I don't locate this missing final piece, the whole family company goes kaput."

A dark shadow crosses Ry's face. I get it, I do. I know what he had to leap through to save it from company hands. Sure, he fell in love and reformed himself because of that, but this shit is so...annoying.

He's in love, but he's still him. "I wouldn't care, but come on. Do you know the kind of boring crap I had to endure?" He shudders. "I have nightmares. Nightmares."

"And Elliot."

Ry glares at Hud. "Of course I have her. I'd have gotten her, anyway."

I know that's just posturing on his part. Of all the things he's ever been sure about, there's only one he wasn't, and that was the redhead who turns out is his match. Ry faltered, questioned himself, and somehow found himself all at the same time. He got the girl—he's Ryder—but that's because he put everything that mattered on the line.

"Uh huh," I say. "You suffered."

His eyes narrow, but he smiles and across the room the young wife of some rich ass sighs. And my brother doesn't even notice. That's how far gone he is. The great Ryder Sinclair who could pick out a willing female at a thousand paces doesn't see the one a few feet from him.

Love.

It's fucking twisted and stupid if you ask me.

Still, he's happy, they all are.

I look at them all. "I've a mind to let it all go, but you've all done so much to get to this point."

"Even with changing fucking rules," says Hud.

Mag takes a sip of his drink. "For reasons not known to any of us."

"We all have our own empires, but that isn't the point. They're saying if it's not there, the company and the inheritance is gone. And, I don't appreciate being fucked with. What's mine is mine and what's coming to me is mine, too."

"So, no luck then?"

I ignore Ryder. And my phone that isn't ringing. "This isn't about money as in actual dollars to dollars. This is about us. We lose the company, it makes us look shaky. It takes away that something extra. I really don't care about the inheritance we all have. I don't need that money."

"But you want it."

"Of course I want it, Hudson. It's mine. And stupid games won't be what takes it. Or the company. I've got feelers out, I'm waiting to hear from a few leads and I've hired the Raven."

Ryder looks at me. "You hired a cat burglar?"

"Ex."

"I'm aware people hire what they think is the Raven, but—"

"It's her."

Ryder's face splits into a wide grin. "Hot?"

"And a cynical, duplicitous woman who's probably going to try and steal from under me."

Ryder looks at Magnus and Hudson. "So, he's saying it's true love."

"Mother also had her name on a scrap of paper. Well, Raven."

Hud smiles. "If she wasn't so annoying with this, I'd admire it all. What is she up to?"

I don't answer because I've no idea at all.

Mag hits Hud on the back. "Speaking of mothers, when's the baby due?"

"You know how these things work, right?" But color snakes up his cheeks. "And how did you know?"

"Scarlett's not drinking booze," says Ryder.

Magnus nods. "All glowing."

"And," I say, "you hover like she's made out of glass." I look at the others. "They haven't told anyone, so heading out of the first trimester."

My brother groans. "I'm in over my head here. But yeah. We're having a baby."

The others start talking all over each other and my phone rings. I make my goodbyes and head out into the early afternoon.

By four p.m., I'm frustrated.

Nothing from Sadie. And she still has my damn watch. I'm still working out how she managed to get the leather band opened and it off me without me noticing.

One thing is for certain, I decide as I head to Jenson's office as I've been summoned, I'm going to have to keep a close eye on Sadie. Work with her. Be her fucking shadow if I have to.

But I want the best.

I also don't appreciate being summoned. The meeting, though, is short and sweet, simply that he went to collect everything as per the instructions from the safe and they were gone. No sign of a break in, nothing.

All I have to do is sign a document stating if the tiara isn't back then the aforementioned loss of the business begins. To prove this is true, he shows me the paperwork on that, signed and dated before my father's death.

To really check, I need a copy and I ask. Jenson tells me he'll forward it to my attorney.

It doesn't matter, though, because my mother has stakes in the company and while she isn't there, she's not about to let it all go on some kind of whim.

Once all that is done, I set out for a walk in the park. I need to think.

The wind is cold and bitter, but the sun warming and the sky clear. The weather's dichotomy reminds me of the push and pull inside me right now.

Part of me wants to tell them to fuck themselves...not that it's Jenson's fault and not that I'd say that to my mother in so many words. She wouldn't be pleased, to put it mildly, and while I'm not in the habit of doing things to please her, I'm also not in the habit of trying to piss her off.

Let's just say the world might think we get our ruthlessness from our father, but the deeper vein is very much from her.

I don't know what she's up to and why she dropped the scrap of paper. Accident? On purpose? Really, I'm not sure it matters because both questions come to the same answer...Faye Sinclair had Sadie Hess on her mind.

The reasonings?

Asking her isn't going to get me anywhere.

I'm just going to have to go into this with eyes very wide open, a heavy serving of suspicion, and keeping Sadie where I can see her.

My phone buzzes and I ignore it. Work. They know I'm taking time away from the day to day so if they're contacting me...

With a sigh, I cut my walk short and pull out my phone.

It's late when I get home. Work idiocy has been averted, and some social drinks that were business in disguise done and dusted and a quick catch up with an old college friend has pushed the hours back further than I intended.

Still nothing from Sadie.

She'd said she'd get to work and be in touch and I'm thinking I don't like that arrangement. I want to be there, too. Going through this each step of the way like I planned. Tomorrow morning I'll call.

When I check my email, I go over the latest information a PI I hired found on break ins to do with jewels—rare, old, coveted, worth a fortune—and art in the last six months. I'd asked if he found a pattern to go back further.

But if what he's sent is a pattern, I'm not seeing it.

There are no signs of the Raven. And the break ins haven't been a few things. They've been sloppy or random.

Unless someone is making it seem that way.

I rub my eyes. With a sigh, I get up and give the notebook I'm making scribbled notes in a disgusted look. Nothing at all. I'd thought maybe I could have something as a starting point, and either work on it with Sadie or see if she'd gone to the same place.

But tomorrow morning I can deal with that. I shower and go to bed.

Something wakes me.

A sound.

Like breathing.

Soft.

And something slow, like a low buzz of electric awareness whispers through my blood. The darkness blankets my bedroom as I pulled the blinds designed to block light.

My heart starts to beat faster, but I just snap on the light and sit up. "There are things called phones. And regular hours. Not to mention doorbells."

"I prefer this." Sadie's leaning against the doorframe, dressed in black, her hair back to hardcore pixie, with the longer side tousled and falling almost over one eye.

"Dramatic?"

"My own terms."

"Aren't you a little old for teenaged rebel bullshit?"

"Aren't you a little young for cantankerous old man crap?"

I grin and go to throw black the quilt. "I'm dressed."

"I've seen it all before, anyway. Men are not as impressive as they think they are."

"You broke in to fuck with my male ego?" I get up and go find some jeans. There's a part of me that wants to just stay in the boxer briefs—she's lucky I wore something tonight—but it's probably not that smart. She's looking all sorts of delicious and sleep still wraps around me with soft edges and the last thing I need is to get an erection.

She'll never let that go.

Figuratively.

I pull them on and turn to her. She's staring at me. My ass, if I'm not mistaken from how high she has to lift her gaze, and how slow she then goes, even as her cheeks start to tinge red.

"Like what you see?"

"Just looking to see where the scars from your implants are," she says with a sniff.

I come up to her and lean on the other side of the frame, crossing my arms over my bare chest. "How did you get in, anyway?"

"I'm very good at what I do. State-of-the-art security is nothing to me. And you didn't turn it on. Just a tip, service entrances are a godsend to a good criminal."

"I'll note that down." I let my gaze slide over her. Christ, she's lovely. "The hour?"

"Maybe I'm into the witching hour?"

"It's past that."

"Call me a tardy witch, then." She turns and starts down my wide hall, her boots silent on the hardwood floors. Me? You can hear me.

Sadie turns right and into my study, turning the light on as she slides behind my desk. My computer's on, spilling its light on the notepad with a vicious scrawl below mine. An expensive pen sits, lid off, letting the ink inside the nib dry. Only the touch of a smile tells me she did that deliberately.

"Fire this guy. Actually, you don't have to. I already did."

"You broke into my email account."

She sighs and spins a little in the leather chair as I throw myself on the sofa opposite the bookcase of boring books that serve me well for various business purposes. I tuck a cushion behind my head.

"I'm afraid my skills don't go in that direction." She smiles a little wider. "Lucky for me you didn't close out your account."

That should make uneasiness sink into my bones, but it doesn't. For some reason, I don't think she came in here to read work emails and personal emails. And if she did, she's going to be disappointed as there's nothing of interest to her in any of them. Nothing juicy.

"Lucky you."

"Aren't you going to ask why I'm here?"

"Aren't you going to tell me?"

She taps her finger on the notepad. "Your detective did bare minimum. Police reports and the like. I've been spending the day looking into other things. Talking to the right people, some of those you'd call the wrong people, and looking at things that aren't reported."

I sit up at that. "What do you mean?"

Talk about the fucking cat who drank the cream.

"What I mean is do you know where the tiara was held? I do. Not Jenson's office. That's his name, right? The lawyer? Well, there are things that haven't been reported. Like that break in. Which was noted. A month ago."

I'm frowning. "That's when my brother told me..."

"So maybe we should start there. What do you say?"

"You know I'm saying yes. But is that it?"

"No," she says. "I have a plan. How about a mini-road trip? See who and what is behind this."

# Chapter Eight

## SADIE

I cast Kingston a glance as I drive the vintage Jag I've borrowed.

He hasn't said much since I picked him up at seven. Not to me, anyway. The first part of the drive through the city towards the Bronx he's on the phone. It sounds boring and work oriented and I tune out. As we hit the start of Hillside Park, he hangs up and rubs a hand over his face.

A different watch glints in the sun. I'm not sure of the make, as I only catch a glimpse and I'm driving, but I smile.

Yeah, I gave him back his Breguet last night, but I expected him not to wear one today. Seems like he wants to taunt me. I've half a mind to steal this one, but I also wouldn't put it past the man to have managed to put on it some kind of alarm.

And stealing his watch means touching him again, something I don't think I should do.

"Sorry about that. Apparently, they can't do without me."

"It's nice someone wants you, Kingston."

"You'd be surprised."

The dryness makes me laugh and I can feel his gaze on me. I don't turn to look at him. Just keep my eyes on the road in the bright and crisp morning sun.

"You're not going to ask where we're going?"

"Not really," he says, "I don't think it's some dark place to kill me, or even some kind of roadhouse to shock me. So I'm thinking…White Plains."

"I could be taking you to Valhalla."

"The town or the Norse place for the dead warriors? But no, White Plains. Some of the most expensive real estate in the country's in White Plains."

He's right, that's exactly where we're going.

"Don't you want to know why?"

"Jenson has a property here. My mother's more Hamptons. Hudson—my brother—owns some things out here, too. But I don't think we're going to any of his properties. What do you want with Jenson?"

The other questions hang heavy in his words.

Questions like what are you up to.

"Not Jenson's place. There's another, owned by Sinclair. It took me a little digging—" which is interesting because this wasn't in anything I discussed with his mother "—to find it."

"You're saying it's not listed?"

"Yes and no."

"Subsidiary." He stops and I can almost hear the frown. "But why would the location of the tiara be some kind of strange secret?"

"I'm not interested in that."

He shifts in the seat. "You know, I never asked if it was reported to the police."

"It wasn't. I looked into it."

This time he doesn't speak for a long time. "It's a test."

I'm almost positive it's a test, but whether it's one that's gotten out of hand, I don't know. Faye's paying me to locate it, and to take my time. She didn't use those words, it was more along the lines of helping her son and not moving things along too fast, after she got me in to look at her security system.

She's very good at whatever game she's playing. And her son? The fewer opinions I form of him the better.

None of these people are my world.

I prefer the fringe.

"There are a lot of reasons not to report things," I say. "Maybe there's a stipulation or maybe it's a matter of the insurance claims not worth it, or a myriad of reasons."

"Or," he says, "A test."

"Yes. Maybe one that's gone wrong."

"Maybe."

I drive along, following the highway to White Plains and the property I found in the digging I did. It might mean something or it might mean nothing. But that old familiar tingle of adrenaline when I stumbled on it says it just might be the former.

"Tell me about the Sinclair jewels. What you know," I say.

"You know it all."

"Humor me. On paper isn't the same as from the heir."

I glance at him and he's studying me. Heat flares hot and needing inside at that look. I turn back to the road, fingers squeezing the wheel.

"My great-great-grandfather had them made for my great-great-grandmother many moons ago. Around the time he made his fortune, and they were, as legend has it, the reason she married him."

"So she was a money-grabbing woman?" I say this before I can stop myself, but Kingston just laughs.

"That's what I said. It didn't please my mother."

I glance at the google maps on my phone. No one has dared put a GPS system of any kind in this car.

"But," he says, continuing, "Mother claims it was a symbol of true love. I'm not really going to argue. And they weren't photographed up close or anything back then and rumor has it he locked them away when she died. Where they remained and faded into rumor. It's not very exciting."

"But rumor is. Stories get big and...things gain value. Especially now your father decided to posthumously release them to you all. Do you know why?"

I glance at him and he shrugs. "My father did what he wanted. And there have been stipulations."

"Up until this last one, which has gone missing."

"Not stolen?"

"No police record, remember? We don't know why. We'd have to ask Jenson and your mother." I tap my fingers against the wheel. We're heading into the big properties outside of White Plains proper. The kind people need copious amounts of money for. "You don't strike me as the kind of man to follow whimsical dreams, especially when they come with hoops and whips and stipulations."

The air in the car thickens with my words and the accidental sexual undertone they carry.

"It depends on who has the whip and the safe word."

Heat climbs my neck and his soft chuckle tells me he hasn't missed that.

"The money," he finally says.

"Cold, hard cash?"

"Come on, drop the censure. You're telling me you did what you did—do what you do—for the beauty of the pieces and now the accolades?"

I pull onto a winding road and drive past manicured lawns and beautifully landscaped grounds, up to a sprawling mansion. I park and turn to him. "Fine, you got me. I like money, too."

"But not as much as me," he says, sliding a little closer to me in his seat and my breath catches in my throat. "Because what? You grew up poor?"

He's touching on a nerve, on something I don't think about if I can help it. But damned if I'm giving him a thing. "I have nothing to do with this."

"My reasons for wanting something that's mine do?"

I lean in to him, my blood hot and moving fast in my veins. "Not at all. Simply working this out."

My heart thrums as he looks at me, those dark blue eyes with the gold and copper striations making something like desire whisper inside.

"Have you worked out why you kissed me if you don't like me?"

His words streak a white heat down my bones. "I told you."

"Curiosity. And I'm not sure I buy it. Maybe it's because we're so alike."

"I'm nothing like you."

"Aren't you?" He slides a finger over my cheek.

The touch is fleeting, and it shakes me. The Jag's small, but somehow it's suddenly grown smaller, tighter, and I want to close the gap. I want to run.

He shouldn't be this observant. He shouldn't look at me like he can see inside, and he shouldn't be hard edged in exactly the right way. The way that turns me on.

"Let's go," I say.

Kingston doesn't answer, just gets out of the car and leaves me to follow.

We're at the door in no time, on the vast, wide verandah and there's a hard-edged expression on his face that suggests he knows exactly who this place belongs to.

He rings the bell and after a few minutes of a strange, awkward silence between us, footsteps grow louder inside and finally, the door opens.

A blonde woman, about forty, looking maybe thirty and well dressed and familiar gives me a once over and then settles, warily, on Kingston.

"I can be here, Kinston," she says, crossing her arms.

She looks like Faye. Not as beautiful, but there are similarities I can't miss.

"Misty. You changed your hair."

"I had an arrangement with your father," she says. "I can live here. It's not like he lacked properties."

"Actually, we're here to look at the pool house," I say.

She blinks at me and a thousand questions crowd her face. "I don't use it. That thing's been locked up for years."

"No problem. I have keys." The lie comes easily.

She sniffs. "Help yourselves."

As we make our way around the house and into the pool yard, the giant covered pool and area, I have to admit, are tasteful. It's a show of wealth from the granite small pool and surrounds, to the carefully curated trees and deck chairs and seated pagoda, but one of quiet confidence instead of flash and bang.

"Your dad's ex-wife?"

"One of them. She got discarded for the younger model he married a few years ago. It was his conceited rich man thing."

"The string of ever younger wives?" I cast him a glance in the crisp air. He's eating up the path we're taking towards two builds. One is clearly the maintenance pool house, another is even smaller and pretty, so I'm betting it's a bathroom and changing area for guests.

I'm interested in the larger building up further.

"You're too late if you're thinking of applying," he says, with acid. "He's dead. And, unfortunately for you, not his type if he lived."

I'm not sure what the acid is aimed at, whether it's me or his father or the string of women. If Kingston wasn't rich in his own right, I'd guess it was because the string of women would eat into his inheritance, but...

No, that's not right. I look at the lean and tall man next to me in dark jeans and black sweater, the expression on his handsome face giving the granite a run for its money. No, even if Kingston wasn't rich in his own right, that wouldn't be the cause of the acid.

He's into money. But he doesn't strike me as that level of entitled. He's not a man who'd sit back and wait for it all to come to him, like he was owed.

If he wasn't rich in his own right, he'd be doing well, or building something.

I shut down that line of thought. I don't need it and it doesn't matter.

"Not something I've been interested in." I come to a stop at the door. It's locked.

I pull out my tools and get to work. Kingston only glances at them and then leans back against the wall. "The one thing I never got is why my mother stayed so loyal, so close to him."

"Through the betrayals? Maybe she left him?"

"I don't remember. They split when Ryder was young. It never felt like that, even when he remarried."

"Maybe," I say, sliding the second tool into the lock, "they loved each other."

He starts laughing. "My father? He loved Sinclair's, he loved his empire and what his children could do, and looking good."

"So, he was a bastard?"

He shrugs. "Aren't most of us?"

The lock snicks and I open the door, the familiar flood of accomplishment running through me. There's enough light coming in through the shutters to see, but I flick the switch next to the door so things are bright.

It's like a giant office. Luxurious in creams and dark woods and it's not for show. It's definitely been used. I head for the desk because I'm curious about this place. I'm not sure Faye knows about the ex-wife staying in the house, or that she'd care. It's none of my business. The job at hand is. And after much digging, Sinclair the elder spent a lot of time here.

In this get away office.

I rifle through work things and letters on the desk. Through files and photos and notes.

"You think the jewels were kept here?"

I pause, hand on the desk drawer. "I don't know. Stands to reason he had them somewhere."

"With Jenson. In a bank vault. The usual suspects."

"Your father thought about them at some point. So, when my digging led me here, I figured it was a good place to start."

Kingston has a portrait, large, gilt-framed, in his hands. It hung over a faux fireplace that's filled with all the pieces made for keeping hearths clean, for stoking the embers. But it's clearly not meant for use.

I know the portrait of Kingston and his brothers as kids hung there because I spotted it when I came in, and there's a wall safe.

"Or he decided to fuck with us from the great beyond."

"Other than holding a séance or finding a signed confession—" I pull open the drawer "—we won't know."

Just neat odds and ends in here. I go through the other drawers but find nothing that's going to help.

"Why not one of his other places? His Manhattan home? The one in the Catskills?"

"Too obvious?" I cross to him as he sets the portrait down. And my gaze goes to the young Kingston. A boy, already with steel in his eyes, and something else, like he's trying to prove something.

I don't need to know about his daddy issues. I have enough of those to last a lifetime.

"I find it interesting he had this place. And he used it."

"If Misty's here, he used it because they spent time here."

I nod and go up to the safe, careful not to touch him. He's a little too disturbing. "Yes, but I get the feeling he used it after they broke up. And he'd come here alone."

"And you get this feeling how?"

I turn a smile on him. "Research. Any chance you know the combination?"

"Aren't you a master thief?" He crosses his arms.

"Don't believe what they tell you in movies. Most safes are broken into by basically blowing them open or cutting them open."

He sighs. And starts trying various combinations.

In the third drawer I opened was a picture. It had marks on it like it had been touched often. Looked at. "Try your mother's birth date."

"Okay, but I don't know wh—" He stops talking as the safe clicks and he meets my gaze.

Electricity shoots high through me.

He opens the door.

"Photos. Some jewelry, documents."

"Give me the photos."

He pulls them out and I take them before he can say a word. Bingo, as they say.

Photo after photo of the jewels. "Are there any evaluation papers?"

Things rustle as I keep studying the pictures. "No."

My fingertips tingle as I run them over a close up of the tiara, the intricate work, the stones. They're the same with the others, but the tiara is the standout.

"I think these are by Mininchi."

"Who?"

"A master jeweler who only did some pieces and stopped. A long time ago. He went in another direction with his art, but the way he worked metal and stones, all designed to be worn, are spectacular, especially the show pieces. There aren't many, and if these are early Mininchi...well..."

"They're worth a lot."

"More than you can think," I say.

He smiles slow. "I can think of a lot."

"I'm sure you can. Someone else must have seen these. If word was somehow out that not only did the Sinclair jewels exist, but they were Mininchi, then..." I look at Kingston. "These are huge. Especially the tiara."

"You have a look. Like you might have a lead."

I shake my head. "No lead." Yet. "But I know someone who's into them."

"Who?"

"My ex."

# Chapter Nine

## KINGSTON

The irrational flash of sharp-edged jealousy isn't something I expect.

There's nothing to be jealous of. I might be physically attracted to her, but it's not like I'm looking for anyone, and if I was, Sadie Hess would not be it.

Of course she's had significant others. She wasn't grown in a test tube or released from some nunnery.

It doesn't help I'm between lovers, and my last relationship of any meaning ended a number of months ago. My life's been too caught up with my work, and now with the fucking bullshit to do with my family.

I quell it. Pushing it away. The jealousy is nothing more than a blip, an inherent kick of my base self, wanting to claim territory because it's there.

I'm not my fucking brother.

She's talking, saying something about going, and part of me agrees. Another part wants to poke around in here, because there's such a feel of the old man and I want to explore it.

I also want to pull the place apart, bare handed.

"Yeah," I say, "we should go."

She's straightening the photos, then gestures to the safe. "If there's nothing else, we should put things back."

I do that, close the door and turn the dial, locking it again. And finally, I put the picture back in place. As we leave, she locks the door behind us and then she looks up at me. Those dark eyes are intense.

"Do you want to see his wife, let her know we're going?"

"Ex-wife. Nope." I never had a problem with Misty, but she's not exactly someone I'd seek out. And my father didn't marry her for her brains or personality." I head back down and around the pool, and out to the Jag. There, I lean against the driver's side.

It's a beautiful piece of machinery and in the cold, clear air, the sun shines down and the deep green of it seems alive with other colors, down in its depths.

I'm not a car guy, but with this, oh, yeah, I could be.

"So." I hold out my hand. "Who's the ex?"

Sadie looks at my hand and then at me. "You don't know him."

"I might."

"You don't. Move."

"I'm driving."

"This isn't my car," she says, scowling at me as the cold air makes her shiver. I know because I feel its bite, too.

"Steal it?"

She tilts her head to one side. "Would it matter?"

"If I get a criminal record, it might."

Sadie shoves me, but I refuse to move. "You're a billionaire, you can make that stuff disappear."

She's probably got a point, but I've never had to try. "I don't think you know how the law works."

"Move."

I'm ready to argue when my work phone rings. I pull it out and sigh. So much for things operating without me. I glance at her. "You're lucky I have to take this."

"Yeah, I'm quaking."

And with that, I go around to the passenger seat and slide in. The car is small, the space overwhelmingly full of Sadie, and I'm too aware of her so the call, cowardly as it is, is the perfect excuse.

I pull out my personal phone and open notes. The drive here set my senses alight. Her scent teased and flirted. A lot of questions swirl, but they can wait until we're in a space with room. A space I'm not locked up so close, where a small movement could result in touching her. Letting the frisson of energy from her to leap along my senses.

Why she has this effect on me is a mystery. I don't like her; she's hostile and a criminal and secretive and the kind of person who fascinates me. There are depths and I don't like her because if I let myself, I would and I don't know what that means except a world of trouble.

I shift my attention to my phone and my executive assistant. "Okay, Holly. Lay it on me."

My call contained a lot of small things with big consequences and it took me the entire forty-five minute drive back to Manhattan to deal with everything.

We pull up near my building and I shift in my seat, fighting the urge to touch Sadie. "As disappointed as you're going to be, I need to take care of this."

She taps her fingers on the steering wheel and studies me for a long moment. "You don't have an NDA or something up your sleeve."

"For what?" I tuck the phones away in my jacket on the seat.

"All the juicy tidbits I overheard."

I start laughing. "If you find all that juicy, you might need to get out more, Sadie."

"I was fascinated." She offers me a small smile.

We both know she wasn't. It was nothing but tiny dry things that need to be done.

"Do you work all the time?"

"I'm on sabbatical. Taking a break."

She frowns. "That's you taking a break? You're doing it wrong."

I sigh. "If I want things to run the way I do, then I need to keep my hand in, even when I'm not doing the day-to-day stuff."

"Isn't there a saying about work smart and not hard?"

"It's not that fascinating and there's nothing to steal. And I'm a control freak in that way. I have people. Great people. People who do certain things better than I ever could. People who do things I can't. This shit..." I shrug. "I can do this. I have to make decisions and delegate. I have to sign off on a lot of things."

"So you don't take time off?"

"I am."

"This isn't time off, Kingston," she says. "It's not being in the office."

"I'll call you later. I have to deal with all this."

And I don't give her a chance to argue, I get out of the Jag and go inside. To work.

It's only sheer will that gets me through it. My mind keeps wandering back to the morning, to the search and why it's important who made the jewelry. The pieces. And why the tiara is the one missing.

I pour a drink. Then set it down. I'm finding my mother's part in this wholly suspicious. That grows with each passing minute.

Maybe I'm wrong. Maybe I'm clutching at anything. But I'll do that. I don't like being used. I don't like being manipulated. I don't like games.

I feel like that's what's happening.

Without another thought, I grab my coat and head out into the early Manhattan evening.

A swift walk across the park really doesn't do much. Not the bite of cold that makes my nose a little sore. Not the freshness the cold lends to the air.

It's not until I'm at my mother's place on Sixty-Third street that I realize what I'm doing. She opens the door on the fifth bang.

"I have a camera," she says, letting me in. "I could see it was you. No need to huff and puff on my door like some kind of beast. I was upstairs getting ready."

I close the door behind me. "Did you know Misty is at Father's place? In White Plains?"

"No, I didn't know." She says this calmly, checking her make up in the eighteenth-century French-style living room. There's an oval mirror in an ornate frame hanging over a delicately carved and polished table. "You came roaring over here to tell tales?"

"So you knew of the place?" I ignore her jab. "In White Plains?"

Faye sighs. "Your father owned a lot of places. He had a number of wives after me." She says this like it's some kind of unknown number as she runs a hand over her perfectly styled hair. Then she looks at me. "Why are you here?"

"Visiting my mother?"

"Kingston..."

I cross my arms. "What are you up to?"

"Excuse me?" she asks after a pointed pause I completely ignore.

"That's why I'm here." I move to the entrance of the room, where behind me the wide hall sits with its dark golden polished floorboards. "You asked, I'm telling. I want to know the answer to that. The what are you up to part."

"I'm heading out for dinner, dear."

She walks up and then stops as I don't move out of her way and a small frown mars her perfectly made up face.

"You know what I'm asking."

"Kingston, if you're that hard up for companionship, you should have called ahead. This is a lady's night and I don't think a group of fifty something and up women are going to do it for you." She gives my arm a squeeze. "Move please."

"No." I don't let her leave her swank apartment on the East Side, where she likes it a little quieter. She has a place on the West side of the park, but uses that for parties and guests she's not overly fond of. I lean against the door in the foyer and annoyance flickers over her face. "Just wondering what your hand in all this is, why you'd want to help Father."

"Because it's complicated. Because regardless of the divorce, we remained close. I have my reasons and I won't be questioned by my son."

"You're making me jump through hoops."

"The tiara is gone, Kingston. No hoops anywhere."

"Did you take it?"

Silence, sharp and heavy, comes down for a handful of seconds and she presses her lips together. "I'll pretend you didn't say that."

"Did you?" This is not the way to speak to her, and I know it, but I don't give a shit. What I want is answers.

What I want is to end this sooner rather than later, because sooner removes the disturbing presence of Sadie from my life. So I wait.

My mother sighs heavily. "I'm not out to sabotage you, if that's what you're thinking."

"I'm thinking there's more to this than I'm seeing."

"There is. And that's for you to work out, Kingston. But I'm not trying to sabotage you or anyone. Find the tiara. That's all I can say." She pauses. "All I know."

But I'm not finished. "You had her name."

She doesn't bother hiding it. "Sadie Hess is the best out there. You seem to have found her on your own. Now, I'm running late."

With a sigh, I step away. I know that tone and I've pushed things further than I should have. And as much as I don't care, she's not going to give me anything else. At least not now. If she knows anything. Which I'm fucking convinced she does. "Come on, I'll walk you to your car."

My mother gives me a tight-lipped look that morphs into a small smile. And takes my offered arm.

Back at my place, I'm not exactly happy. A caged lion paces within, throwing off my equilibrium. I've been trying to find things from the other people I have out there. And on my way home, I contacted my PI, the one Sadie told me to fire.

I stop and sip my bourbon.

Jenson.

That's who I asked him to look into, along with Misty.

The woman's at the house, so it seems like a good place to start, but there are others. My father's divorce settlement gave her everything she asked for, everything she could in the confines of their pre nup. But he was generous by his standards, and Misty has been seen with some top surgeon in White Plains, so that explains a lot. She's always struck me as someone who defines herself by having a partner, and I don't think she has it in her to know the value of the tiara and to steal it. Then again...

Stranger things have happened.

But I just got a call.

Nothing on Misty.

Jenson on the other hand...

He has debt.

A lot.

And he's a man who can cover that with his firm until he can't.

Jenson is also in the perfect position to set it up. To steal.

Question is, how desperate is he?

I'm going to need to find out.

# Chapter Ten

## SADIE

Damon's handsome face isn't smiling as he sees me.

I narrow my eyes as I look at him across his desk. Of course, I let myself into his office, but usually this has never bothered him.

There was a time that it turned Damon Reed on.

"Sadie." There's something in his tone that sets off a warning inside me, like I've caught him, hand deep in a cookie jar. "I didn't expect you."

It's the kind of tone that says he's been doing exactly that, expecting me, and not looking forward to it at all. I smile at my ex.

"It's been a while, I thought we should catch up." I lean forward in his chair and motion for him to take a seat opposite. "What are you feeling guilty about?"

"Me?"

I point. "You."

He has the grace to turn red. "I haven't cheated on you."

"It's a little hard to do when we broke up five years ago. Of course, you did, then."

"Sadie," he says, "you want to talk about this now? I spent a year chasing after you. A year apologizing, pleading, arguing. A year trying to tell you what you walked in on wasn't what you thought."

He's probably right about that. Sure, some hot chick was all over him, but clothes were on. And he's a good-looking man. He might not be in the realm of the dark hotness that's Kingston Sinclair, but Damon's blond beauty is very easy on the eye.

"You should have cheated on me," I say suddenly. "I wasn't the best girlfriend."

"You didn't love me like I loved you, but again, I don't think you're here to rehash the past, so why bring it up?"

"Actually," I say, "you did. I just asked what you were feeling guilty about. It's all over you."

I've seen Damon use his skills and brains for both good and the slightly evil. I've seen him manipulate. I've seen him help others. So, I'm not sure why he never quite did it for me. Why I jumped on the concept of him cheating as a way out of the relationship.

I'm not made for long term, and he is, and I know that. But he's the kind of man a woman wants. I know that, too.

Kingston, on the other hand...

I don't like his kind. He fascinates me, and I'm not sure why. Kingston somehow gets inside and stays. He's smart and hard and cynical and he disturbs my equilibrium in a way no one else ever has. It's something I want to hate the man for.

Instead, I shove Kingston out of my brain, as much as I can. And I push the folder of photos across Damon's desk.

"What's that?"

"It's not a bomb, Damon," I say. "Let's call it a blast from your past."

I lied to Kingston. Damon's no thief. He's in security. High end bespoke stuff. I hand jobs to him after evaluating. The good jobs. We're at the point I can just send him the number and report and he steps in.

But regardless of how it ended, those fences have been patched and I don't think he loved me as much as he thinks he did. My reputation and the idea was more appealing than the girl. And he's gone on to really make a name for himself. People know about the Raven. They don't know about Damon beyond his security company.

Which drags me back to why he seemed so guilty, but I decide to bide my time before circling to that again.

"If you're asking me to fence something or arrange a meeting, I can't."

"You mean you won't."

He takes his seat and the folder, but doesn't open it. "Yeah, I won't, Sadie. I've worked hard to get to this place. I'm legit and there comes a time you get out of shit, and you know that."

"That's why I do what I do and get you work."

His gaze flickers at me, but he's wise and keeps his mouth shut. Instead, he opens the folder and hisses in a breath.

For the next few minutes, he studies the photos in silence, but there's a thickening in the air, and the way he sits up straight and focuses like a laser on the pictures tells me everything.

"So it's true..."

"Are they real?"

He looks at me. "I'd have to see them in person. If they're not, then they're brilliant. Mininchi wasn't the only one in his family who designed and made jewels. But he had a way with them. And these look early, a light touch. Sinclair, aren't they?"

It's not really a question. "I don't have the final piece. It's missing."

"I didn't take it."

"I'm not saying you did, but interesting you went there."

He frowns. "You're the kind of person who thinks everyone's involved until you can prove they're not."

"I don't usually chase down stolen things."

"You used to be the one stealing them, that's why." But there's no rancor in his voice.

"Stolen," I say, "or deliberately missing."

"What do you mean?"

"I'm here because I wanted a list of who'd be interested. Not the usual suspects, the hardcore collectors with real ties in certain circles. And why you gave my name to Faye Sinclair."

He nods. "It isn't a crime." Damon runs a hand over his face. "How did you know?"

"I know when Damon Reed's put in security," I say. "You have a certain way with your work, one I can spot. And don't worry, I don't think anyone else can. It's just...you."

"I'm flattered."

"Use that flattery wave and tell me everything you know."

Some might think the Bowery, back when it was full of the homeless and punks or now where it's full of the rich, is a strange place for someone to have a security firm. But it's perfect. It's still a crossroads area, and Damon can keep things on the downlow, which is what a lot of his clientele like.

Not because they're up to something, although some are, but because it allows those who want to keep their business to themselves to do so. Especially those who want something other than just security.

Like me, Damon knows a lot of people. And that includes, well, people like me.

So, my question is this: did Faye Sinclair go to him to find me specifically, in a way that was below the radar to her peers and children deliberately, or did the missing jewel spark it?

I have a lot of questions.

My fingers itch to call Kingston to discuss it. My body yearns for that.

My brain says no.

So I head to the source.

Faye herself.

"I'm not sure," Faye Sinclair says in her home office on the East Side, "that you coming here is a good idea."

"I saw your security man, Damon Reed, today."

She rests her chin in her hand. "How is that working on the job at hand?"

"I like to explore all options."

"I'm not paying you to do that," she says, sitting back and dropping both hands on her desk.

I come up and sit on the edge of the desk. It's borderline insolence, but there's a gleam in her eyes as she takes me in and it reminds me of her son. It tells me she's also a force and one that shouldn't be ever taken at face value.

"Yes, but you don't want the tiara gone. Do you?"

"Of course not. I have my reasons for wanting it dragged out and Kingston hiring you on his own is perfect."

I don't move. It's not that she knows, it's how she says it, like there's another plan she's had, and somehow I've stepped into it. I shake off the thought.

"You've both told me there's a lot riding on this."

"There is. Kingston is…" She sighs and gets up. "I worry about him. He's so self-contained, so certain his way is right, that there's nothing more than making money and he classes value in one way."

"A lot of people do," I say, choosing my words carefully. "He's interesting."

"You and he will clash, which is good."

"Is it? I'm here to both keep him from finding this jewel too soon and helping him find it. But you know where it is."

"I don't think I can state enough how important this is that Kingston gets this done by his birthday. There's a lot more on the line than he thinks."

I nod, not quite sure what she's up to, if anything at all. "Like what?"

"My hands are tied, but he stands to lose everything dear to him."

"This is a conversation you should be having with him." I rise and walk along the desk, coming up to the same end she is. Except, of course, I'm on the other side. "Not me."

"I'm letting you know because he can't. He needs to work out that out on his own. The tiara needs to be found and he needs…" She shakes her head and smiles, even though it only flirts with her eyes. "He needs to go on a sharp learning curve."

"You make it sound like he needs a babysitter, not someone who's an expert in tracking and finding jewels and stolen artifacts."

It's one way of putting it, I suppose.

She looks at me. "You're the right person for the job."

I don't care what Faye Sinclair is up to. I don't. And it's her son we're talking about, not someone she's out to get revenge on. Whatever cards or games she's playing aren't any of my business. I need to do the job I'm here to do.

And if I dig deeper, locate the tiara ahead of her schedule, there's no need to do anything about it, like tell Kingston.

If I want to get it forged, then...I'll make that decision when I find the damn thing.

One thing I'd like to know is why she sought me out. In particular. I know why Kingston did. But his mother could have chosen one or a dozen people. Because I don't think notoriety is high on her list of skills.

I'm the best in many ways, yes; but she wants a babysitter, a watchdog. She wants PI with who's going to yes ma'am her.

I'm not any of that.

And my ex knows all of that, too.

"You know..." I glance about the room. At the over the top security most people, including most thieves, would miss. "This security is interesting."

"I'm rich. We need to protect our things."

I nod. "I know how it works. But you..." I gesture in the room. "You have taste and no need to show off with exceptionally showy pieces that are either collector items or easily taken to sell on the underground market. Yet you went to a bespoke security firm. You don't need it."

"You really are a match to my son," she says. The smile stays, and grows. I'm immediately intrigued and suspicious. "I don't need it, but I want it."

"Or you went to Damon to get information on me."

"Why would I do that?"

"The match."

Her eyes narrow and the smile falls away. "Kingston will trample most people into dust. I needed the right person for the job. Yes. But, he did find you on his own without a push, so maybe there's hope—"

"For what?" The words come out sharper than I mean.

"That the jewel will be discovered." There's real amusement behind the steel of her look. "Now, Sadie, please do your job, the one I hired you for."

"And Kingston, too."

"If you're worried about the morality of the situation, don't be. Kingston is all grown up."

I know she's layered her words with a subtext I don't get. Or is that subtext one I don't want to get? Maybe they're the same things.

"He wants it found."

"Not," she says gently, "for the right reasons. And that's going to be on him in the end. But follow the plan and do the job."

"Do you know where the tiara is?"

His mother studies me. "Why are you so interested, Sadie? Beyond the obvious."

"There's only the obvious."

"If you say so. Is there anything else?"

Yes, so many things, but I just say, "No."

"Good. I'll be in touch if anything changes."

My Yia-yia—she's not my grandparent by birth, but she's the woman who saved me in so many ways, took me in when I stared the down the barrel of a future that would have swallowed me down, and taught me to believe in myself—is tapping her foot in her Harlem home.

Her improbably dyed black hair, stacked heels, and take on mourning dress that would give any fashionista a run for her money is one of the many things I love about Mrs. Athena Diakos.

I flicker a gaze at her from where I'm sitting on her too comfortable red sofa. "Sorry?"

"Does he have a name?"

"Who?" My cheeks burn.

She pops a fist on her left hip. "The man distracting you."

"Not a man." And Kingston really needs to get out of my head on my time off. "It's a job."

"Right, and I'm twenty-five, not forty."

She's seventy if she's a day, but I don't say a word.

"This job that doesn't involve the man you're not thinking about, it's above board?"

I frown. Thing is, I want to tell her about the deep layers of unease inside, but I don't know what they're from. I want to tell her all the ways Kingston infiltrates my blood, but I don't know how. And yeah, a part of me wants to whisper to her that I kissed him and want to do it all over again.

I don't do any of that. Instead, I meet her gaze. "Of course. I don't do any of that anymore." Even though, I admit to myself, I'm tempted. "It's been years."

And it has. Rumors have had a way of building me into something way more dangerous, way more criminal than I was. Not that I didn't take from the rich. I should rob Kingston blind. I'm not going to. He'd come down hard, bring his own brand of retribution and...I don't fear it.

A small thrill threads like sparks through my veins.

No. I don't fear it. I want it.

Shit. What's wrong with me?

"Does it have to do with the whispers I've heard?" My Yia-yia asks.

My head snaps up. "What whispers?"

"Sadie, I've heard things." She folds her worn hands with the vixen red nails in front of her, face a sudden study in worry. "And with you, I usually don't. Not unless it's all the boring above board gossip."

"That's all it is." Unease snakes through me, even though it's true, even though I want my hands on a Sinclair jewel. Want and thought isn't the same and carrying through. "This is just more above board boring gossip."

"Sadie..."

"I'm locating a missing item. Doing my thing."

She doesn't speak for a few moments. "Let's just say I've heard you're looking for a certain tiara with a certain billionaire."

"I don't like Kingston Sinclair." The words are out before I can stop them.

"And I'm the grand Queen of Sheba." She sits next to me and takes my hand. "Because I didn't ask that."

I draw in a breath, scrabbling to save face. "You don't have to. I know you."

"And I know you, dear." She looks down at her hands and then at me. "You're about to tell me you're fine on your own. Don't be alone."

"I'm not."

She goes to say something, but doesn't.

Out of everyone, she knows me the best. She worries, I know she does, but I'm fine. I like my life. And I especially like it man-free.

"There's something else," I say, "isn't there?"

"If I've heard, so has he."

We don't say my father's name. "I haven't been under his influence since you took me in."

"Honey." She squeezes my hand. "He might have lost out on molding you into his partner in crime, and you would have been a better con artist than him, if you chose that path, but he's not above blackmail, and if he hears you've an in with a billionaire."

"I've been working for the rich for a long time now, Yia-yia," I say. "This is no different."

"We're talking Sinclairs. We're talking *the* tiara, Sadie. And he's a greedy, manipulative man."

"One who's in prison."

"One whose parole comes up in a few months."

"And I'll be finished with the job. It's short term."

"Short term has a way of getting away from you, Sadie."

I switch the subject to the latest man she's had her sights on. Though she knows what I'm doing, she lets the other conversation go. For now.

Athena is one of the strongest women I know. She got out of a terrible marriage, she got out of a worse relationship. She did things she won't talk about, and things she will. She's saved so many young people in terrible lives because she wanted to. She wasn't ever rich, but you knew her place was a safe place.

And I owe her.

Everything.

I give her what I can in a way that's never insulting. She does well, but I know every bit I give, everything I can do, goes to help her help others. And, out of everyone in this world, I love her.

It shames me in the time I was with Damon I never introduced them because she meant more to me than him. Because I didn't want to share her.

But there's only so long you can eat her delicious homemade cakes and drink tea or ouzo if she breaks that out and I set out to work, making my goodbyes.

As I take the subway downtown, I'm caught up in my thoughts, so caught up I almost miss the transfer at Forty-Second Street to the F. But soon enough I emerge at the Second Avenue stop, and as I cross the streets, down to Avenue A and my home, I admit I hate the idea of my father being free.

Yia-Yia is right. He'll turn up. I should have kept up with it, and I now will. Forewarned is good.

I'm staring down at the pavement as I walk, turning to my building and I run into him before I can stop myself.

Strong hands that heat my skin and flesh grab me and I look up into that darkly, devastatingly handsome face. His evocative scent wrapping about me.

"You never answer your fucking phone," Kingston says.

I don't want him to let me go. "No one makes calls. You're behind the times."

"Smart ass."

"Stalker."

His mouth twitches, but he doesn't smile and he releases me. Then he steps back, and pulls a photo from his inner coat pocket and holds it up.

"We need to talk."

Fuck.

It's a picture of twelve-year-old me.

And my father.

# Chapter Eleven

## KINGSTON

Sadie turns pale and takes a step back.

Not the reaction I expected, but then again what about her is expected?

Certainly not the fact her father's a fucking hard core con man. Her last name is different. But that doesn't matter. I never looked that deep into her. At least not delving into parental lineage. There's nothing linking them.

Nothing, that is, but the photo.

It's old, and that's her. Long dark hair, perma-scowl that barely hides fear and vulnerability. Skinny and gangly, and a pretty kid.

I don't remember this moment in time, as I was fourteen, but I know who he is. The con man, Mr. Sweet, the papers all called him. He preyed on the vulnerable, bilked people out of their money and homes. Sweet? Not at all. He was the worst.

It would be easy to call the man a bottom feeder, a thug, but he wasn't. Since the photo surfaced in my hands, I looked into him.

He's ruthless, lacking in morals, savage, and what some might call a sociopath, but I call a soulless criminal.

Trevor Masters. Serving a twenty-year sentence for his crimes.

Sadie's father.

"Where did you get that?"

"I was going through the information from my previous investigations into criminals who stole jewels." I flip the photo toward me a moment. "Now I know you, it's not hard to see who that is."

"You don't know me." She doesn't spit the words. She doesn't hiss or yell or snarl. They're quiet and soft and they hurt something in my chest and make the breath catch in my throat.

"Runs in the family."

Her eyes now flash fire and she snatches the photo, crumpling it. "No. It does not. I'm not him. Nothing like him. At all."

She pushes past me and I let her, the night sky heavy above, the air cold and damp with the promise of rain. A few people passing by glance our way but I ignore them, everything tuned into the vibrations of her.

Sadie opens the door and steps into a dusty, dirty old foyer, complete with flickering fluorescent light above and old pizza flyers on the floor with discarded junk mail.

The building though, with the tin roof and details on the cornices, is something that would look spectacular if stripped of years of old paint and chip board.

I'm aware I'm doing this on a base level so I don't have to think about the change in Sadie, so I don't need to feel the tight knot low in my gut.

But I follow her. Through one door and then up a staircase to the second floor, where she opens a door and goes inside. I stop the door with my booted foot and push it open.

"What part of me trying to slam the door in your face do you not understand?"

I step inside. "The same part that isn't finished yet."

"I think we are."

"I'm not going anywhere."

"I'm not in the mood," she says, snapping on a light.

And I don't move.

It's not huge. But it's beautiful. A clean, wide space that managed to be cozy with white oak floors, a small wood and steel table near one of the windows, and a fat sofa and chairs around a shelf of books and a mounted flatscreen that has a pile of books on the fireplace it hangs over. A big plant sits in the space where fire should burn.

Other rooms lead off, three. A kitchen, bedroom, and bathroom no doubt.

It's not the place of someone who's grown rich from others, but it's had money and love and time put into it.

A haven, I think suddenly. That's what it feels like.

"It's also not for sale." Sadie crosses her arms and glares.

"You need to stay in touch with me."

"When there's something to talk about. And this photo is not such a subject."

I sigh and rub a hand over my face. "I came here because...."

The words stop. I'm not sure why I came here. Except maybe I wanted to see her, be near her.

Because I need to keep an eye on her. That's why. That's the only reason. End of story. And now I know her father is a big bad criminal I—

"I'm sorry."

Her eyebrows rise. "You're sorry? For what?"

"Bringing the photo."

"You're sorry for bringing something up you clearly came here to bring up?" She laughs and the go fuck you tone does a good job of hiding the hurt. Good, but not great. Because I can see it, smell it, and I don't really know what to do with it. "No, you're not."

"No." I guess I'm not. "Are you working with him?"

She stares at me like I've slapped her. Hard.

I don't think she is, but I didn't get to where I am, I didn't get to be me, without questioning things. And I'm attracted to her. I learned long ago, with that woman, the one I fell for, that attraction makes us blind. Vulnerable. Stupid.

And I'm not a stupid man.

She's the exact kind of woman I never thought I'd meet or want. And that's how cons work. Finding the in.

"Excuse me?"

"You heard me, Sadie. I've a right to know."

"You have no rights with me except you getting your fucking tiara. I bet after you milk it, you'll sell it to the highest bidder."

"No, I'd want you to do it for me."

"Why? So you can get the highest price?"

I glare and stalk up to her. "And so what if I want that?"

"You don't get what it is you have with the tiara." Her eyes narrow. "Rich people."

"Says the criminal."

"Ex."

"And I have a right to know who and what I'm working with," I say, her scent of jasmine and smoke with its wisp of spice winding around me, drawing me into her. "It's one thing working with someone who steals from the rich and insured. It's another working with someone who destroys lives."

Her dark eyes glitter. "I'm no fan of my father, but how is what he did different from what you and your kind do to people?"

"I don't take from people who can't afford it. I don't destroy lives. And I don't do it deliberately with no thought about anything except myself."

She turns away and I catch her arm, her flesh warm beneath the coat. We both look down at my hand and then at each other. And the sparks leap and dance and tease. "I'm not him."

"What am I meant to think?" The situation is slipping free from my fingers, but the fire burns down into my bones. That flame between us that ignited the moment I saw her. The moment I tasted her dark sweetness.

I'm mad she's evading me. I'm annoyed at myself for sliding a knife in between ribs. And I'm fucking turned on.

So is she.

It heats the air.

"You're not meant to, Kingston. You hired me to do a job, and I'm doing that job."

"We're doing it together."

"I work alone."

"We work together. Especially now I know what runs in your blood."

Silence bites and she shifts, sliding in closer, brushing against my body. "The same murky tendrils of morals that runs in yours?"

"We're not the same."

Sadie laughs, looking up at me, contempt and desire a dark and fascinating war in her gaze.

"You might have billions, Kingston, but you're not any better than me." Her mouth turns in a cold semblance of a smile. "The difference, apart from being handed money on your end, is you'll do anything and everything to get by, to build a world for yourself because you can. I do it because I have to."

I frown. "Don't play games with me. I don't steal."

"Don't you? Mr. Billionaire?"

Letting go of her arm, I hook mine around her, drawing her hard and flush against me and she makes a small sound that's primal, full of need, and grabs my cock. Desire burns fast and I'm hard. I want her. More than anything.

"You have a way of sliding about things, Sadie. Like the fact your name was with my mother. Like the fact you're doing this." I whisper the fingers of my free hand against her cheek. She's like heated silk.

Her hand comes up, and curls in against the lapel of my jacket. But she's not pushing, she's holding and we're pressed together, a throbbing beat of need. I want her. The understanding—it's beyond thought—comes again, and I want her so fucking much it's a physical ache inside.

"And you have a way of pissing me off." She whispers the words, a world of desire caught in them. "You don't leave me be."

"No," I say, that same desire thick and rich in my own voice, "that's you."

"I don't..." She trails off, rising on her toes, her mouth a brush of air against mine and the heat inside flares, making my guts tighten, my cock harder.

She looks at me, a mere inch from kissing, and she's a fuck you, she's a dare. She's vulnerable and hard. She's push and pull and I understand everything in that gaze because it pulses inside me, too.

Right or wrong, good idea or bad, I'm going to taste her again. I lower my mouth, her heat coursing through me, but suddenly she moves, turning her head and pushing and I stumble back.

I'm both grateful and resentful at her cowardly, smart move.

"I don't think that's something we should do."

"No," I say. "I agree."

"I don't like you," she says.

"Preaching to my fucking choir." I look her up and down and she's breathing hard. So am I. "But we're working together. Like has nothing to do with it. Or want. Because we have that, too. And Sadie? When it comes to work? We do everything together. And you tell me everything. Got it?"

"Like it's made of glass." Sadie's mouth curls upwards. "You don't trust me."

"I don't trust anyone."

And I leave.

Outside in the cold air with the humid touch that says rain, I shove my hands in my pockets and head over to the East Village, my steps biting the ground as I cross in front of traffic and plow through people.

I ignore the shouts and horns.

My phone buzzes in my pocket as I reach the bar where I'm meeting my brothers and their partners. I pull it out and look.

Mother. I read it and shove it away.

It's easy to find them at the corner of the down-to-earth bar, a far cry from the usual haunt of Ryder. But he looks happy, smiling and laughing at something Elliot says. She's good for him, and...yeah. I get a drink from the bar and go to them, slumping down in a seat.

"What's got you in knots?"

I glare at Magnus. "This bullshit non-quest."

"You don't give a fuck about that."

"I do when it comes down to losing everything in regards to the flagship company."

"Yeah, well..." He looks like he wants to say something, but looks over at Zoey and rubs the back of his neck and offers me a sheepish grin. "Maybe I'm not the right person to ask."

"Why do you look like life is hard?" Ryder asks.

Hudson nods. "Agreed."

"You lot, leave your brother alone." This is Scarlett.

Elliot laughs. "They won't."

"Are you okay, Kingston?" asks Zoey, who is way too sweet for black-hearted Magnus, but she loves him anyway.

I just shrug. "Mother's up to something." I shake my phone, then grab my drink, finishing it. "She's full of dire warnings about how I have to do this right."

And then there's Sadie. Hot, difficult, intriguing Sadie. A woman who won't leave me the fuck alone, not even when I sleep.

I'm going to have to do something about that.

Like get this job done and dusted as soon as I can. And yeah, get her to sell the shit out of the heirloom so it won't remind me of her.

I order another drink and tell my family to leave talk of quests and dead fathers and manipulative mothers alone for the evening.

I'm a little drunk when I finally leave, the liquid warmth of the booze making me feel loose as the world loses its sharp edges. I could get a car home, but I need some air and though it's spitting fat drops of rain here and there, I start walking.

The hour is late and I stayed past when my brothers left. I stayed and flicked away all and any unwanted attention that came my way from a few willing women. They weren't my type.

They weren't Sadie.

I shove my hands in my pockets as I turn onto East Sixth street and falter.

A strange coldness grabs the base of my spine.

I'm not alone.

Someone is following me.

# Chapter Twelve

## SADIE

"Normal people," Kingston says as he turns like he knew I was there the entire time, "just say hello. Or call."

"Dinosaurs make calls."

His mouth twitches and heat streaks through me, the now-familiar pull to him swooping through my system. "It's not all texts and emails."

"No, it's phone calls and carrier pigeons."

This time, Kingston laughs and he leans against a wall, the cold intermittent rain giving the city a shine, giving him one, too. And he takes me in, his mouth soft, generous, and the most sensuous thing I've ever somehow managed to turn down.

I don't know if that makes me an idiot or smart.

There's a softness about him, not just his mouth; all of him. "Are you drunk?"

"No. But I'm human."

"Are you?"

"I had a few drinks. Why are you following me?"

"Not following," I say, keeping my distance from him because to do anything else would be me launching myself at him and claiming that kiss I denied earlier...something I can't do. I'm not that self-destructive. "Looking."

Kingston nods, like he knows.

Of course he does. I'm good but I'm not magic. I came after him when he left for reasons I don't understand. And I sat at a bar opposite the one he was at, near the window, working and watching to see what he did next. I could have gone in to the one he was at, but this man has an uncanny ability to know I'm there. Like he's tuned in.

He's smart, and he's someone who is highly aware, but it's like he's got a special radar for me.

Like the one I have for him.

I ignore that thought.

"So, you were looking for me?"

Suddenly he straightens and that hard edge starts to slide back into place.

"Yes." I put on a cool tone to match his.

While watching him, something popped up in my messages from Damon. But I don't say this.

"I thought we could talk."

He nods and then he whips out his phone. "Let's get out of this rain and go somewhere to talk, then."

This part of East Sixth is residential, but bars and restaurants in the East Village, West Village, and Lower East Side abound.

"Okay."

I'm curious. That's the only reason I slide into the black car with him when it turns up. It's why I don't ask where we're going. That becomes obvious as we head across town.

He cuts a look at me. "Don't think you've gotten lucky."

"And here I wore my best underwear."

"I'd prefer you not wearing any."

Silence engulfs us for a beat and my entire being sings and tingles with pleasure and need from his words.

Kingston doesn't apologize, and his dark blue eyes burn hot.

"I..." I can't think of a thing to say because my head is suddenly filled with fantasies of him, naked.

"I just thought if you figure we should talk, I figure we should do it somewhere private and comfortable."

"Sounds like a plan."

I follow him into his building, riding the too small elevator—how can one man take up so much space, so much air, so much of my attention?—to his mansion in the sky.

Like the time I broke in it grabs with the fact it's livable. I see so many rich people's places that are generic showrooms or so over the top it's hard to breathe for fear of breaking some gaudy and insanely expensive thing.

His place, with him, makes it real. I'm not sure if that's the right word, but it fits. The place is Kingston. Oh, there are expensive pieces, but everything has its place, everything is built for comfort and to last. Clean lines, masculine without hitting someone over the head.

"Cataloging?"

I turn and narrow my eyes. "You've got a mouth on you, Kingston. One that might get you in trouble."

"Depends on the trouble," he says, dumping his coat on a chair and kicking off his shoes. He closes in and eases the lapels of my jacket from my shoulders. "If it's your kind of trouble, I might be interested in seeing where it leads."

I swallow and step back, the glint in his gaze doing dark things to me. Shrugging the leather from my shoulders, I dump it. On the floor. And he laughs.

"No one dares speak like you do to me. Or does shit like that. Most people would be...solicitous..."

"To be in your sacred sanctum?"

"That's one way to put it." Kingston moves off and to a bar, one of those old-fashioned carts, but this one clean, strong lines in wood and smoked glass, and dark sheening metal. It shouldn't work, but it does. I'm guessing a bespoke design for him. "You have a chip on your shoulders, big as Texas."

"That's some chip." I cast my gaze to the modern art painting on the wall. It's real and it's worth a fortune. It fits the room, too. The strong reds are offset with the black and grays in it. The mood it gives is at once sensual and austere. Hard line or hot sex, that's what it says to me.

"I get it, Sadie. You don't like rich people. And yes, it's real."

"You know I know that. That artist's turned his hand to other things. This piece is worth a fortune and going up in price."

He laughs as I turn. "And you know I know that. Why the chip?"

"I don't like the rich."

"Why?"

I shrug. "I've told you a lot of the reasons."

"Indulge me." He picks up a bottle of amber liquid in a plain decanter and turns it in his hands.

I take a step forward and stop, on the middle of the living room floor, between the sofas and lick my lips. "I don't know. I guess so many have a sociopathic edge."

This isn't necessarily true. But those who do, and the way so many go about fleecing others because they can even when they have enough, it reminds me of my father, and how Dad has those genes.

It worries me that I might be the same.

Even though I'm not.

"Stupid things," I add. "You're different than I thought."

"Too much or not enough of a sociopath for you?"

He sets down the decanter and opens it.

"Well, you haven't kicked me out for not kissing up to you," I say.

His gaze meets mine. "I find you both a pain in my fucking ass and completely refreshing." He picks up a glass. "That what people do?"

I don't pretend not to understand him as outside rain begins to hit the window in earnest. "I'm treated as a circus attraction."

"You don't have to do it, you know. Work for these people you don't like."

Smiling, I spread my hands. "Where else am I going to rob them legally? They don't need me, not most of them."

"And me?"

"I'm still figuring that out. But," I say, "I want to see that Sinclair piece."

"I'll take that." Kingston pours some drinks, crosses the room and hands one to me. "Whiskey neat. I can get ice if you'd like. Or a mixer."

"No thanks. I'm grown. I can handle it."

"Can you?"

"Yes."

The heat flares in his eyes and he smiles, soft and small and cat like. I should be nervous the way he looks at me, like prey, but I'm not. It sends thrills shooting through my veins and makes me want to throw down more, just to see what happens.

Instead, I accept the drink and his fingers slide deliberately against my skin.

"Sit. Take off your damn boots." He nods at the nearest sofa as he steps back.

Taking a swallow of the whiskey, I deliberately sit on the floor.

Kingston laughs and drops down next to me, setting his glass next to mine. "You always do that? Deliberately poke bears?"

"Maybe you bring it out in me."

"Maybe I do." He starts undoing the laces of my boots, and there's something intimate about it. I should stop him. I don't.

"Would you prefer I grovel, Kingston?"

"Hell no." He eases off one boot. "I like how you are."

He tosses the boot over his shoulder and it lands with a thud. Then he does the same with the other.

I'm not exactly sure what's happening, but...I think I might like how he is, too. He's a pain, he's hot, he's smart, he's intriguing and different from anyone I've met before, and he makes every single part of me buzz.

"You have lovely feet." He traces a finger down over the top of my foot in the black sock. "But you didn't come here to discuss your feet. Since you are here..." Kingston tosses down his drink and I grab mine and do the same. "I wanted to say sorry."

"For what?"

He gets up and comes back with the decanter. "Coming at you about your father. We can't choose our parents."

"You don't like yours?"

Kingston pours us both another drink. "No, I do. I love them. My mother's interfering and loving and devious and the old man was a workaholic. I just mean we're ourselves and they're them and you don't go around conning people."

"But I do. That's what my job is with the evaluations."

He raises his glass and a brow. "No, I'd say you give them what they want. And you know what I meant."

"I don't want to talk about him."

For a moment I think Kingston's going to argue with me, but instead he nods. "Okay, how about a game?"

"What do you mean?"

"You give nothing away for free and I respect that. I do." He stretches his long legs out as he sits opposite me, then raises his glass. "So, a game. We each ask the other a question."

"Is this a drinking game?" My insides tighten at the way he looks at me.

He smiles. "Yes. We take turns in asking questions and answering. Say I ask you a question and you answer, I get to guess if it's truth or lie, and—"

"Truth or dare?"

"Truth or lie, Sadie. I guess right, you drink; I guess wrong, I drink."

"You think I'm going to say no, don't you? But what if I back up the lie with a lie?"

"Will you?" he asks.

"I might."

"You won't." He takes a sip of his drink. "And if you do? I'll know you're lying."

I narrow my eyes at him and lean in. "And if you back up a lie with a lie? Or a truth with a lie?"

"I won't."

I grab his chin with one hand, his stubble the right amount of rough against my fingertips and it does things to me. That combination of hard, soft, heat, and scratch. I want to feel it against my bare flesh. I want his face—mouth—between my thighs.

The thought should shock and make me run.

I stay exactly where I am.

"I'll know if you lie, Kingston."

He moves, sliding his cheek against me and I drop my hand. "So?"

I could con him, win this. After all, I learned how to twist lies into truths to my own advantage from the best. But I'm not going to do that. "You're on. I'll start. How old are you?"

"You're not trying. You stole my wallet."

My mouth twitches as I try not to smile at the mock serious expression on his face. But his eyes...he knows the base part of me, how I can't back down, and this is definitely a challenge. "I'm setting a baseline."

He breathes out, gaze hot. "Thirty-five. Almost thirty-six."

"True."

He only looks at me and has a swallow of his whiskey. "Your illustrious career on the other side of the law. You said it was exaggerated. You want me to think it isn't, I think it is. Am I right?"

I stare at him. I could lie and he wouldn't know, he—

"Right now, you're thinking of a way out of an answer."

He's bluffing, I'm sure of it. "Just mulling it over."

"No mulling."

"Rules on rules?"

"They're like Russian dolls."

I want to laugh, but I take that sip. I point at him with my glass. "Why is all this so important to you?"

"That's not yes and no." He slides a hand over his thigh and my mouth goes dry. "And I told you. I want what's mine."

"You asked me to sell it for you."

"Yeah? But I want it first. I want to know what it's worth and then we can do that. I want what's mine. That's why it's important. I want what's mine."

I hesitate. He does, I know that, but I don't know what else is there, motivating him beyond what he told me. And how he looks at me when he says that... "Okay, what about love? Do you believe in love?"

"Why, Sadie," he says, mocking me, "Do you have a heart?"

"You can't answer with an answer."

"No."

I stare at him and he stares back, not reacting. Finally, I take a sip. "Something we can agree on."

"Are you an only child, Sadie?"

"Yes."

He just smiles and takes a sip.

"You think you know me, Kingston?"

"Not at all; that's why we're doing this."

"You know what I mean. You think you know the truth about me?"

"Yes." He lifts his glass. "You need to drink. You skipped."

"You're cheating. You keep asking things." I take a savage swallow. "And you went and took my turn. You don't play fair."

He finishes his drink. "Of course I don't. Where's the fun in that?"

"Why do you really want to find the tiara?" I need to find familiar footing. A safe place. This seems about as safe as it gets.

"I told you." He looks at me. "Money."

"Truth." I finish my drink and he refills it. I'm aware he's a little tipsy, just at the edges, but I don't make the mistake of thinking he's any less dangerous than he usually is. I stop and consider my thoughts. Dangerous? Yes, he is, in ways I can't quite define.

"And you?"

"Money," I say.

He doesn't drink. "This is where we both have a sip. Because I'm both right and you're lying."

"You're drunker than I thought."

"I'm not drunk," he says. "You're in it for money and thrills. Are you going to steal it?"

"You're not playing fair."

"Answer."

"It's my turn."

"Answer," he says, his voice soft.

Am I? Yes. No. I don't really know. So I say that. "I don't know."

"Truth." And he has another sip.

"Why did you really take me to your place?"

"To talk."

I point at him. "Lie."

He stares into his drink a moment, then at me. "Thing is, I keep fighting it, but..." Now he lifts those blue eyes to mine. "I want to kiss you, Sadie. Do you want me to kiss you?"

Everything stills. Then my heart starts to beat hard. "Yes."

We're not playing anymore. And I don't know why I said that. I don't like backing down from challenges, but I'm not stupid. I go to take a drink when his hand comes down on mine and he takes my glass from me. He's so close his breath warms my lips.

And then he kisses me.

It's soft, sweet, and almost not there and I crave more. This time, I return the favor, and his mouth is perfect on mine. Again and again we tease each other, my stomach swirling, dipping, flying and he makes a sound.

I don't know what it is. A low thing, almost like a sigh. I might not know, but my body does, and it's like a dam breaks within, and need and passion come tumbling out and I wrap my fingers into his shirt, bringing him in.

He kisses me, hot and urgent. Mouth open, tongue there, and I let him in. I kiss back with the same deep hunger. It sweeps through me. And kiss tumbles into kiss.

We're wrapped about each other, his hand on my cheek, my throat, against the side of my breast and then my waist as we roll into each other.

I'm drowning, more of this and I'll be naked in his arms and I'll forget why I came here.

That's the only reason I end the kiss.

Not fear or a dark wave of the prospect of losing myself in him, because like I'm going to do that.

Somehow, I find it in me to pull free, untangle from him.

Struggling, I manage to find my breath if not my center. "I had a reason."

He sits back, dark gaze on me. "Pardon?"

"For coming here."

"And you remembered now?"

"I got distracted."

A smile touches his mouth. "So I see."

I can still feel his kiss. I can feel the slight burn from the stubble, the softness of his lips. The heat of his mouth and the slide of his tongue.

"I have a lead on the tiara."

# Chapter Thirteen

## KINGSTON

I'm aware her bringing up the lead was nothing more than a way to get out of the kiss last night, and I'm glad.

At least, I think I'm glad. Because who knows where that stupid drinking game I came up with might have led if I hadn't gotten distracted by her.

It's still raining the next evening when I stare up at her apartment.

This isn't part of her plan, but fuck that.

I ring her buzzer and it takes a while before she buzzes me in without asking who it is.

That tells me she knows it's me. She's probably got security up the wazoo. That means she's got reasons to watch things closely, or she's got a secret room packed full of jewels and treasures from many heists.

Though the pirate booty room appeals to a part of me I didn't know existed, I'm betting it's the former.

She leans against her open door when I arrive on her floor. Sadie's arms are crossed. Her expression might well be a universe from the woman I kissed and who kissed me last night, and I'm glad. I think.

Glad because it shouldn't have happened. I had too many drinks and let my guard down. Glad because kissing her is disturbing in the most lose yourself, lead into the best sex ever, and more kind of way. It's the more part that worries me.

Yet I want more.

"We're meeting later, not now." Her voice is cool and calm.

"You follow me last night, drop a bombshell, and then walk away," I say, coming in close because I want to shake that cool and calm right out of her and bring about the high stakes buzz of awareness that's inside me to her.

Something I suspect is there. Hidden away.

"I said what I needed to say."

"Right before you ran off." I deliberately drop my gaze to her pretty mouth. "Like a scared child."

"I didn't run." She turns and steps inside and I follow, closing the door behind me. The rain hits the window opposite and a trickle of water runs down my nape. Serves me right standing outside without an umbrella.

I lean against the door, my hands in my jacket pockets as I contemplate her. She really is beautiful, the dark hair of her pixie cut curling in the dampness, her eyes big and blazing now, even if her expression is one of placid disinterest.

I'm giving her room to move, to get some rope, to step into the untested darkness I can feel beckoning at the edges.

She takes the bait and storms up to me, stopping short of me touching her even though I make no move to do so. "I didn't run. I said what I came to say and I left. There's a difference."

"After we kissed."

"So?"

I consider her gauntlet. "So," I say, "I guess I'm curious why you didn't tell me you got a lead that the tiara was going to be fenced, as you put it."

"I did."

"Not straight away."

She offers me a tight smile. "I got distracted."

"Well," I say softly, "that's good to know."

Sadie spins away from me and goes over to a small desk and toys with her phone. She sighs. "I've been waiting on word, confirmation on this so-called sale."

I straighten and cross to her. "You don't think it's for sale?"

"I didn't say that. My gut instinct is whoever is supposedly behind this is merely trying to whip up interest in it."

She watches me and a coldness spreads. "You're waiting for me to finger point at you? Like a double bluff?"

"Are you going to do that?"

Am I? It's not really something I've thought about beyond the bare bones. Is she capable of it? Absolutely. Would she fuck me over? That I don't know. "Call the cops? No."

The words are out and she nods. "It could be me behind all this, pulling some kind of double bluff con."

"You could. I'm sure you're capable of it."

Her phone lights up. And she reads whatever comes up and puts it down. "I think this is a way for someone to get information and garner interest. Like I said."

"Then maybe we need to find out more."

"Maybe we do." Her gaze melds with mine. "That was word it's on. How do you feel about Coney Island?"

I just smile.

It's cold out at the old beachside crumbling attractions that must have been something back in the day. Now things are old and tired and gaudy.

But there's something about Coney at night during the off-season that gives it something. If I were a romantic, I'd say it added to the tarnished aesthetic that gives it character. But it's just old and empty.

Mostly empty.

I'm curious about where this is headed. Sadie told me some things on the trip here, in some old car she claims she borrowed.

We're in an arcade that's closed for the off-season. It's dark and cold and perfect for sitting close to share body warmth.

"This isn't very exciting," she says.

I cast her a long look. "I don't know. I can think of ways to make it exciting."

"We don't like each other."

"Who said anything about like, Sadie?" But I don't say anything more.

She doesn't fidget, though the tightness to her hands says she wants to. "As I said, this isn't actually going to be a sale. They usually happen one of two ways; someone has stolen for another person, has a buyer in mind. Or...there's going to be a big thing made of it."

And she's leaning toward the second. "So the latter it is."

"Probably." She shifts, and her breath puffs out in a wispy cloud of vapor. "This could take a while."

"Tonight?"

She shrugs. "That, too."

I consider her words. Across the street is a bar. It's tiny, dank-looking and not like Ruby's that is the star of Coney Island. We're off a Surf Avenue side street, and though we're still in Brooklyn and people live and play and work in the area, we might well be transported somewhere else for the whole desolate feel it all has.

Time's running slowly out. I know that. We're not that far in, but four weeks isn't long. "You worried about me?"

Sadie doesn't look at me as she smiles. "I'm worried I won't get paid."

"Your larcenous, greedy heart appeals to a man like me, so be careful."

"You don't believe in love, Kingston, I'm safe."

I laugh. "Neither do you, and who said anything about love?"

Her cheeks darken, but her smile doesn't waver. "Just making sure you're not going to fall for me. I'm not sure I've got the time to chase you away, stomp your heart to pieces."

I laugh again, delighted. If she keeps going, I might really end up liking her. "That sounds a lot like commitment."

"And you're sounding like you lost your mind." She slides a look at me. "If it's the latter—with the tiara—it really could take longer than four weeks."

"By setting up a big sale, you mean?"

"Gathering all the potentials together, yeah. You tease it out, let the word spread. Honestly, if it was the former, I'd have heard something solid long before all this, that the most expensive Sinclair piece was wanted." She pauses, like there's other things on her mind. "Both could work on similar lines, but..."

"If it was the former, someone would have contacted you to steal it, you mean?"

She shakes her head. "Maybe if there was someone out there with that kind of hard on for it making the rounds. No, I just mean I'd have heard the moment it was gone and I haven't. That's why I think the fencing is a lie and someone is trying to orchestrate some kind of big auction."

I let what she's saying and not saying wash through me.

Like the fact someone would have had to know where it was. "Let's say this was some kind of opportunistic robbery. There's no police report I'm aware of."

"There isn't one I'm aware of either."

We look at each other. "Inside job?"

"You tell me. And while you're at it, if it is, as in someone from the inner circle and not a thief who's worked this from the moment the Sinclair ring confirmed the existence of the rest of the jewels, who do you think stands the most to gain?"

"I don't know."

And I don't. Because this is more than just standing to gain with making money, this has the potential of bringing down the Sinclair family company. There are no stipulations about it being stolen, just it needs to be there on my birthday.

It's convoluted, stupid, and regardless of what it could be worth, this tiara is fast becoming something complicated and maybe only worth selling.

Once I find out the value.

"We should have brought popcorn."

"To watch people go in and out of a bar?" Sadie asks.

I half smile. "I've seen slower foreign art films that make even less sense."

"Philistine."

She shivers and I shift my chair closer. The darkness in here is broken only by the light from outside. The rain has stopped for now, but I could sit with her, doing nothing for a long time and I suspect it would be by far the most exciting and interesting thing I'd done in a while.

"So, apart from your winning personality, Sadie, why don't you have friends?"

"I have friends," she says. "And I didn't have to buy them, like you."

My smile grows. "You were young when your father went to prison."

"If you want to have sex again, I'd stop this line of questions."

"Is that you propositioning me?"

"Threatening."

"Pity," I mutter. "I could do with a distraction from all this bullshit of mother shaped suspicions and manipulative ghostly hands from the great beyond."

"What's your plan?"

This time I don't pretend to misunderstand. "The same. Get the tiara back, stop the damn company from being dissolved and..." I stop. "But getting it back is the goal. Where is this lead?"

"I told you, this is some kind of meeting. I was told here, and I'm not sure who will turn up. Or even if this is going to happen. That's why I wanted to meet you tonight. Later. After I did this."

"And let you get in on the action?" I ask, trying not to shiver. It's cold and my hair is still damp. Still, a few heated moments with Sadie would make me forget all about that.

What am I even thinking? I might want her, but it's a terrible idea. One I keep veering right back into.

Sadie gives me a steady, long look and it's colder than the air. "If you think that's my plan, you're an idiot. There are much easier ways to make money, and all of them far more pleasant. After all, they wouldn't have anything to do with you."

I just start laughing and I shake my head. "Who told you?"

"My ex."

My laughter dies. I don't like the scrape against bones her words have. "Close?"

"Yes. And it's not what you think. Damon heard word, that's all."

I go to say something when she grabs my arm, sending sparks shooting through me.

"That's him," she says.

I look over and an unassuming man in a worn coat and balding head steps into the bar. "Who is it?"

"Saul Weathers. He's a liaison, usually between buyers and sellers. But sometimes he whips up interest."

"How do you know the difference?"

"You don't." She settles back, looking down at her hand and snatching it back. "Not until invites are handed out."

Fuck this shit. I'm ready to go in there when she's no longer pretending to be relaxed. The door opens and this Saul comes out of the bar and Sadie's sitting forward, everything in her vibrating with tension. "Or he does this."

"What?"

"He's going to make a deal."

We follow. It's not too far, Sheepshead Bay, this time a small apartment. Sadie tells me to wait here in the damn car, but I'm doing nothing of the sort.

"This is stupid, Kingston," she says.

I hook her arm through mine, hauling her close. "Yes, it is. Very much so. But sometimes you have to be stupid."

"You don't have a plan—"

"Do you? Other than more watching, waiting, doing nothing at all?"

She tries to tug her arm free, but I close my fingers over hers, holding her there. "I know what I'm doing—"

Sadie stops and turns into me, pressing up and throwing her arms around me, tugging my head down to hers. "Be quiet, they're coming out."

I want to kiss her again. All my resolve melts into nothing and the urge beats like a drum in my veins.

"Damn, this is about a painting."

I realize they're talking, but I don't hear a thing about a painting. They're discussing the weather and temperatures. Code. I'd bet my ass on it.

The two men part and Saul heads our way. I brush my mouth against Sadie's. "Go with it." And spin her into him.

I hope like hell she gets what I'm doing.

Or else Sinclair's might be about to go down the tubes.

Because of me.

# Chapter Fourteen

## SADIE

I'm so furious I'm shaking.

Not even the smoothness of Kingston's inner criminal can soothe my soul as he makes his apologies to Saul.

He keeps my head buried against his chest, a place I like being, which only serves to fuel the fury already burning in my blood to apocalyptic levels of flame.

"Sorry, sorry," he says to Saul again as I tuck the man's phone and wallet into Kingston's pocket.

And then he leads me off and I deliberately slam my foot down on his as we approach the car on the side street.

We get in, but we don't go anywhere. I tap my fingers against the wheel.

"I'd drive off," he says, "but you don't trust me with this heap of junk."

"Because you're an idiot. A reckless, fucking idiot."

"Why don't you tell me how you really feel?"

"I'm getting started," I say. "You're—"

"Sadie, what did you get?"

I huff out a breath. "His wallet and phone, which he'll know are missing right now."

"That doesn't give us much time to find out what's on the phone."

"What's on the—" I stop, and glare at Kingston's austerely gorgeous features. "We're not going to get into the phone and the wallet will be stripped clean. He's not an amateur."

In the light of the streetlamp outside the car Kingston just smiles. "You search the wallet, and give me the phone."

"You're not going to get into it."

"So? Give it to me." He holds out his hand and I slap it into his palm.

Rage rolls through me again, so I focus on the wallet. It's empty. Just cash and a few fake IDs all in the name of Jonas Smith. Well, at least he went as far as not going for John, I suppose. I turn to barrage the billionaire next to me when I go still.

His face is lit by the blue-white light of the screen and he's reading something on it. Then he tosses me the phone.

There are texts from unknown numbers. They seem boring, but one thing jumps out. Numbers and a word.

I look at Kingston, whose expression can only be described as smug. "Well?"

"I think I'll let you live."

Enough time has passed that we can drive off—we leave too soon and we're a target to be followed—and I do just that.

"Do your windows open?"

"I have a terrace," he says. We're in his mansion in the sky. "I'm heavier than I look if you're thinking of throwing me off."

"Pity."

"Besides, kill me and I'll come back and haunt you." He isn't bothered by my inferred threat and his smooth charm tries to win me over.

I don't want to be won.

I'm still furious. And light murder might be on my mind. It's either that or shove him against the wall and fuck him.

Both have their merits.

I take a breath and spin to face him, hands on hips, making sure to keep my distance. "What were you thinking?"

"I was thinking we need to do something."

"That was risky, Kingston."

He stalks up to me. "You thrive on risk."

"You don't know me."

"Tell me," he says softly against my ear, closing the gap between us, "I'm wrong."

"It was a risk." I glare up at him.

He takes a step back. "A calculated one. I didn't get to where I am without knowing how to read a room, or people. And I certainly didn't get here by playing it safe."

I cross my arms. "And here I thought you got to where you are by virtue of your silver spoon birth."

"Sadie, you're trying to rile me up to lead me off the path, aren't you?"

"No."

He's right, I am. Because what I got from those texts wasn't nothing.

"Liar."

I breathe out and go to the sofa and sit. And try not to think about last night and what happened against that one. His mouth felt so good, so right, on mine.

Deliberately, I shift my mind from those earth shattering kisses to the phone. Date, time, address.

I know who is at that address, and it wouldn't take much to tell Kingston. I'm going to have to, because this man has killer instincts. He knows when something is up. "Fine. I just don't want you taking matters into your own hands."

"That's what I have you for." He smiles. It's the kind of smile that makes my stomach flip. It's dark and predatory and it turns me on.

"You don't have me. I'm working for you."

"Same thing."

I sigh. "You found something. Happy?"

"Very." He sits opposite and crosses his legs and my gaze is drawn to them clad in black denim. I might hate him for being so damn hot.

I grip the arm of the sofa and imagine it's his neck. Of course, the image that comes to mind is not one of violence, but one of erotically charged—

"The crap on the phone? It isn't crap. I know what it all is."

"And?"

Breathing out, trying to keep those delicious, disturbing images out of my head, I continue. "It's a time and a date and an address further uptown, in Harlem."

He doesn't say anything, just waits and it's like nails on a blackboard, that waiting, because it's so loaded and I don't like where it's going. And if I reveal everything, just how bad it makes me look.

Not that I've done anything.

At least, not for a long time. And not to him.

"There's a collector. Very rich, maybe even as rich as you."

"Do I know him? Or her?"

"Him," I say, "and no, you don't. This is not a circle you move in, Kingston. You have to understand that."

"You'd be surprised by the circles I move in."

"This man is very connected. And he loves fine art, jewels, whatever is rare and wanted, and if it's stolen? He thinks it's better that way."

I know this man. I've known him for too long. My father goes a long way back with him. My relationship is just in selling the man things when Dad used to make me steal for him. But I haven't seen Mr. Duante for years. When I had my short-lived career, I kept away from people like him. Oh, I saw him around, but that history from my younger years always makes my skin crawl, even though the man has never been anything but nice to me.

Nice because he wanted me to work for him.

That's neither here nor there. He's a way in and I have to go alone. Problem is, I'm not sure I can do this without Kingston insisting on coming along.

I don't want them to meet.

Kingston nods. "Okay. But there's something else. It's in your eyes. You have a brilliant poker face, but I can read you. And I know you're not telling me something."

"I think I should go in alone to see. This kind of word-of-mouth event...it'll be a party...isn't something you should go to."

He nods with a soft smile, one that offers the illusion of agreement, and I know immediately I've said the wrong thing. I've piqued his interest. He's not any different from the rest of his kind. They all want to get a thrill from rubbing shoulders with the likes of me, and what's a bigger thrill than rubbing shoulders with a very rich man with mafia connections?

Kingston leans forward. "Sadie?"

"Yes?"

"If you think for one minute I'm letting you go in alone to face some scumbag without me, you're insane."

"I get it. The idea is thrilling—"

"No." Kingston's voice doesn't change from the soft tone, but the steel there that's made of ice jars me, pins me down to the spot. "I don't think it's thrilling at all. I think it's dangerous and I'm not letting you go alone."

"I'm not the one who'll be in danger, Mr. Moneybags."

"Don't fuck with me, Sadie."

"I'm not." I'm leaning forward, too, but my nails are digging into the sofa's arm and I'm vibrating. "This guy isn't going to talk to me if you're there."

"I'm not a fucking cop."

"You're a known billionaire."

And that's another mistake I make. And he knows it.

"Exactly." Kingston smiles again. It doesn't reach his eyes. "I'm what he wants. Someone with money—"

"He either has or is after the tiara. Your tiara. You see my point?"

"What I see is you trying to tell me I can't go and that's not an actual option."

"You're deliberately being an idiot."

"Me being there will drive up the price," he says. "After all, the whole bullshit with my father isn't known."

"The jewels aren't exactly known."

He leans back, looking completely at ease. "My brothers don't appreciate the value of what they have, only the sentimentality. The jewels are known because they've given them to their other halves."

Kingston says this like it's a crime.

So, I switch my line of argument to another truth. "You're what he wants, but not how you think. This man can grift, and you like money. He can offer you wild riches—"

"Are you trying to turn me off going or head straight to the front of the queue?" Smiles are gone and now he just closes his eyes a moment, pinching the bridge of his nose. Then he looks at me. "I'm not in the market for inflated prices and I'm not looking to start an illegal art collection. Cold, hard money is my thing, not the value of inflated prices that hinge on the whims of others."

There's something heart breaking about that, even though I understand it and agree. I think it's how he says it, like there's nothing else the world has to offer but black and white numbers and dollar signs.

"I can't talk you out of it?"

"No."

I nod. There's one thing I can do. I rise. "I'll be in touch about the event."

"It's in two days. Harlem, like you said. And I remember all the details. I can get there whether you take me or not."

"I know."

And then I leave.

That night I can't sleep. I try to tell myself Kingston's a grown man, but I can't shake the horrible premonition of terrible things if he meets Duante in that setting. No one's going to die, that's not Duante. He's connected, but he's into the money side. If heads roll in his other businesses, he turns a blind eye.

No, I'm not worried about Kingston's life. I'm worried about Duante taking from him. Of finding a way.

That makes me feel like an idiot, thinking someone as savvy and sharp as Kingston would fall for that, but Duante is a different breed than Kingston deals with and I...

I'm protecting myself and protecting him.

My business relies on me having a glamorous, dark edge that isn't sordid in the wrong ways.

If word gets out I'm suddenly rubbing shoulders with Kingston and Duante, then my career could tumble.

Me being there alone is one thing. I can blend and disappear. Being there with Kingston? That isn't happening. And there are people who straddle both worlds.

No, better I do this. Protect myself by protecting Kingston.

And that's the real reason.

With that firmly in mind, a plan in my head, I close my eyes and go to sleep.

It's early in the morning when I ring the bell on the townhouse in Harlem's Sugar Hill. This isn't far from Athena's but it's a different world.

The woman who answers the door is beautiful, snotty, and probably knows how to kill with one hand. I just smile.

"Tell Duante the Raven is here."

Her attitude doesn't change, but she gestures for me to come in and I'm led down through a beautiful wide hall to a waiting room. It was probably a parlor back in the day, but as lovingly restored as it is, the room is clearly designated for people to wait in.

It doesn't take long for Duante to appear.

The man is short and trim and only his eyes with their hungry, greedy gaze gives him away for the kind of lowlife he is. "Little Sadie."

"Let's cut through the bullshit." I don't smile. "I know you're after the Sinclair tiara."

Excitement lights his gaze. "I'm listening."

My heart sinks at the eagerness in his words. He doesn't have it. That's what his little party is about, trying to get whoever took it to sell it to him. Shit.

I keep my shell of calm. "I'm looking for it, too."

"Any leads? To own an actual Sinclair…" He doesn't finish, just clasps his hands.

It would be so much easier for me if he had it. But of course, that's not how life works.

"I'm here to make you a deal."

"Still listening," Duante says to me, eyeing me with a hard look. "What are you after?"

"Anything you hear, pass along to me. Leave the actual Sinclair family alone, and…" I take a breath, and I smile. "And when I find it, it's yours. For a finder's fee."

"Deal," he says.

# Chapter Fifteen

## KINGSTON

The speed with which Sadie hightailed it out of my place yesterday means she's up to something. What is anyone's guess, but I'm not about to have her use her tricky little ways and freeze me out of anything. She works for me, not the other way around. The event is tomorrow night and I'm going.

I don't give a shit what she says.

Actually, I'm insulted she thinks I can't take care of myself. Or her.

Fuck, I'd told her I wanted to keep her safe and—

Did I?

Something happening to her isn't on my agenda. Not at all. But I'd said it like I'd meant it, like I cared and... I don't trust her.

Right? That's the real reason I said all that.

I'm also the fucking tooth fairy. Wanting her safe and not trusting her don't have to cancel each other out. Everything about her says don't trust, just by nature of what she did for a living, who her father is, but...

She's smart and fun and tough as nails. Things which don't mean she can't get hurt.

I'm at my home office, working on some things, when my phone rings. I'm expecting mother to call me back so I just hit answer.

"And here I thought you'd have someone to answer your phone."

I smile at the richness of Sadie's voice. "And here I thought only dinosaurs made calls."

"Just call me your friendly velociraptor."

"I'm not sure they were friendly." I doodle on a pad next to my computer. There are a lot of things I want to say to her, but I'm not going to. "Would you call them friendly?"

"Take it as a warning then."

I start to laugh, then stop. "Why are you calling?"

"The event has been cancelled."

"And I should trust you?" I ask. "Why?"

She gives an impatient sigh. "You're a clever boy. I'm sure you can find a way to either prove or disprove my statement. Or, I can come hold your hand this evening."

"I'll see you tonight." And I hang up before I can say anything else.

My day doesn't go according to plan. There's some bullshit at the office I need to take care of, which I do. If I wasn't so caught up in the dire situation of the damn tiara and who the hell is behind it, I'd find it amusing the fact workers scatter when I walk in.

I know I demand absolute excellence and hard work, and I also know I pay them for it. The old adage of the boss being away and mice playing is applicable everywhere. My mice play on a different level, and they still work fucking hard when I'm not there.

Excellence is something I demand in every business transaction I embark on, and the Sadie thing is no different. Question is, I don't think she's giving me that. Scratch the thought, actually. She is. But she has ulterior motives, and one of those might be getting her to use that excellence as a way to stymie the job.

I'm talking in circles in my brain.

If she doesn't turn up tonight, I'm heading out that door to the meeting she's claimed has been called off. And then I'll be visiting my mother, whom I most certainly don't trust. But right now, I have to meet Jenson. I shut down my computer and I let my assistant know to contact me if anything comes up and then I'm gone.

The sky is heavy and there's been talk of early snow this year, but that really isn't bothering me. No. What's bothering me is the tiara crap.

Because that's tied up with an ex-cat burglar with mesmerizing eyes and a mouth that haunts my dreams.

I get in my car. "Henry and Co," I say to my driver. It's a little restaurant on the east side of Central Park, and I'm going to be late. Something I abhor, but I can't do much about.

Sadie Hess shouldn't haunt my dreams. It's the first time a woman has in a long time. Not since...well, not since I was that stupid kid who thought love was real.

It's probably the tiara business that's putting her front and center. Of course, that works right up until I get to the hot fantasies that star her.

I'm not a man given to fantasies. If I want and the woman is willing, then it happens. No need for fantasies, hot or otherwise.

So why Sadie? She's not my type. Is she?

That bothers me. She's there, under my skin, so deep I can feel her sliding against the bone. We are a lot alike, I know that, but I'm not exactly looking for another me. Not that I'm looking.

We arrive at the curb and I get out, my driver moving off to find a place to park. I head in to the swank little bistro in bronze and red and pale honeyed wood. I slide into my seat opposite Jenson and I'm half surprised not to see my mother there. After all, she seems to have her fingers in everything these days.

I run a cool gaze over Jenson, who seems like the place is too warm for him. He's not sweating, but there's a definite sheen.

"What's up?"

He plays with his menu. "I take it the search isn't going well?"

"I'm not sure yet."

"Time's running out, Kingston, and when it comes to the company, I can't wiggle out of it."

I narrow my eyes. I should be meeting my brothers for lunch, but the meeting with Jenson seemed more important, and that feeling grows with his discomfort that borders on desperation.

"I get all that. But can you tell me how it went missing?" I pause, giving him time to answer, but it's there in his eyes. He doesn't know.

The waiter comes and I order the house salad and croque madame. Jenson the house salad only, which tells me a whole story.

"So, you don't know, and no one reported it."

"Things aren't that easy, Kingston."

I nod and smile. "Things never are." I pause again. "Just one thing; just how much of this is my mother's interference?"

I get home later than I'd have liked. There's work waiting for me. I've three messages affirming that, but I walked home, across the park because the bite in the air helps clear my head.

Jenson never answered me, which told me even more.

I don't think the tiara is meant to be missing. At least not like it is. Perhaps I'm meant to be on some wild goose chase, but if so, I can't see to what ends.

I absolutely know my mother is up to her elegant neck in whatever the fuck is going on. His not answering answered that.

And Sadie's involvement? It might have my mother's prints on it, or perhaps not. That's the thing. Yes, mother had the word Raven written down, but that's exactly the direction she would turn to if the police weren't to be involved.

I honestly don't know what that means. Only that perhaps my father stipulated that.

I don't have answers. I don't have anything, and I'm not sure I want them.

What I do want is the tiara and the money it's worth. And I want to keep the family business private. Yes, for me, but mainly for my brothers. I get something out of it, but they get more, in terms of sentimentality and the fact it belongs to us.

I'll get the tiara in time. Have it valued and Sadie sell it. And then I'll get to the bottom of this mess.

Something isn't right when I let myself into my home. The lights come on as I step in, just like I've set them. But it doesn't feel empty. My cleaning service isn't due for another few days and the air doesn't hang with that sparkle fresh scent from scrubbing things that don't need to be scrubbed.

I stand still in the wide hall and set down my coat and keys. Hesitating, I glance at the phone in my hand and then set it down, too.

No, it doesn't feel empty. Or just vacated. Someone is here.

And I know exactly how she tastes.

"When I said I'll see you tonight, Sadie," I call out as I go into the library and fix myself a drink, taking a seat on one of the leather sofas, the reading lamp casting a soft warm glow and fuzzing the edges of shadows. I take a sip of the Scotch—I like quality single malt when I read—and set it down on the book I've been reading when I have the time. Honestly, it feels forever. "When I said that, I envisaged you on the other side of the door. Or down in the foyer, asking to be buzzed up by the doorman."

"Where's the fun in that?" She comes in, barefooted like this is her home and something strikes me deep at that thought, of what it means and how she seems to fit almost perfectly.

I say almost because I don't like her.

If I cling to that lie, all will be safe and fine.

"Manners aren't meant to be fun."

She makes a scoffing sound and comes to sit next to me, leaning over to steal my drink.

"That is disgusting."

"That," I say, easing the glass from her fingers, trying to ignore that lingering buzz from where her breasts brushed me fleetingly, "is Laiphroaig Lore. Single malt? You need to develop good taste, Sadie."

"Yes, I do. Especially since I'm here."

"Why are you here?"

"I didn't learn anything new today," she says, stretching and sitting back, shifting so she's got a little distance between us. Like that will keep her safe. "And you commanded it. I'm on your dime, Kingston."

I take her in, her cheeks still a little bright from the cold, the tip of her nose a charming pink. "Not been here long, then?"

"Arrived about five minutes before you."

"We're an interesting pair, aren't we?" These words come of their own accord, because we're a puzzle I can't quit. "You annoy me. I annoy you."

"I don't respect you and your kind," she says.

"Right back at you there, Sadie. You're a criminal."

"Now you're being boring and repeating yourself. Ex criminal."

I sip my drink, aware her mouth was right where mine was. There's a smudge from lip balm that tastes faintly of honey.

And of her.

"And yet," I continue, gazing at her, taking in the slight tenseness that comes to her, the dilation of her pupils when she looks at me as she waits. "I don't think I've wanted someone more."

"That me?"

"Just like you want me."

She opens her mouth and the air thickens, but she closes it again and I can almost see her run.

"Neither of us are inclined to do anything about it," I say.

She narrows her eyes. "That would be stupid."

"Agreed."

If I closed the gap right now, I could have her. We both know it. That knowledge pulses in the air like a living thing. I want her. I can't deny that. I've been fighting it since I first saw her. And maybe dislike is wrong. Maybe it's to do with trust. I don't trust her.

But that doesn't bother me, either.

Because I don't hand out trust. Not often and not easily.

No, it's something else I can't quite define, something that goes down to the core of me.

So, I don't do anything.

Sadie unwinds herself from the sofa and goes to the bar area and she grabs the reposado tequila and pours a healthy shot. Then she turns to me.

"Kingston?" she asks, voice quiet, "ever think about looking into your mother?"

# Chapter Sixteen

## SADIE

"Do you want to explain yourself?" he asks after a moment's silence.

There's no censure in his voice, no anger. Just mild curiosity. Everything in me goes on high alert at that.

"I meant—"

"I know what you meant, Sadie," Kingston says, stretching his long legs out in front of him. He's wearing a suit. No doubt one that's bespoke. And it's devastating on him.

I'm beginning to think he's just devastatingly gorgeous, no matter what he wears. But this one does things to a woman. It's blue. Not banker blue. This is the darkest midnight blue that both manages to be classic and have an edge that's utterly him.

Jesus. Next I'll be waxing lyrical over his shoes. Or cufflinks, or— I stop.

"I've been thinking about why the tiara went missing in the first place."

"Someone was careless?" He shrugs. "You tell me. You're also working for her. You're not the first. She hired my brother Ryder's fiancée. Although for completely different things. Elliot's not a high-end society criminal."

I come back around to him and sit again. I don't want to. I want to go stand at the other end of the library. Or in another room. Or another apartment. In another building.

And he knows that. So I sit next to him.

"You don't think it's odd?"

"The end result is the same. And yeah, I was thinking about this walking here after lunch with Jenson."

I dip my head down, trying not to smile. He's the billionaire who walks through Central Park in the early hours of the evening. He's the billionaire I somehow forget is richer than all the gods. He's an enigma in so many ways. Like, why do I want him so desperately?

That's something I've been fighting. Something I didn't know I was fighting, not on the level I have been, not until he said something to me a few minutes ago.

"That," I say, "is the perk of being rich."

"Walking?"

I laugh. "No, asshole, hours long lunches."

"I'm pretty sure there are more perks than that," he says, sarcasm rife in his words. "You should dream bigger, Sadie."

"Did I mention you were an asshole?"

"I think so."

Damn it. I like him like this. I force my mind back to why I'm here. Why I came early. I didn't think he'd take as long from lunch to here, then again, I also didn't think he'd walk.

"I had a late lunch because I had to drop in my office."

"I know."

He doesn't answer for a long moment and my cheeks heat. "Have you been following me, Sadie?"

"Keeping an eye on you." I glare at him and take a swallow of the tequila that's the smoothest tequila I've ever had. "I don't trust you." He doesn't say a word. "You're the kind of rich idiot—"

"Asshole."

"—who'll barge in somewhere wearing too stupid to live badges."

"I gave those up for lent."

My mouth twitches, but I will myself not to smile. "You really are a Class A asshole."

"Everyone needs to be good at something."

This time I laugh. It bursts free and he grins, looking all levels of pleased with himself.

Then his smile vanishes. "How much is she paying you?"

My laughter dries up. And I look at him.

The air between us thrums.

"Would it matter if she is paying me?"

"Is she?"

"That would be telling. And the answer to that really needs to come from your mother."

He sighs and puts his drink down. "That really depends on a few things. Like the capacity in which she hired you. If she's trying to make me miss the deadline by hiring you to throw me off the scent, then I'd say that would matter."

"I just asked if you've looked into her."

This time, his smile is dark and electric. "You're a smart woman, Sadie."

"I don't shoot myself in my own foot. From what you've told me about this whole thing, your mother trying to stop you finding the tiara would hurt you." Faye's words rush back at me. I'm to hold him up, yes, not stop him finding it.

"The company doesn't mean shit to me, beyond what it can bring my name and smooth out certain paths. But I don't need that. I'm already more than successful. And my mother knows I'm not really one for being fucked over."

I shiver as he gives me a pointed look. I'm not scared, but the type of implicit threat hidden in his words sends a frisson of excitement through my veins that's more dangerous than any strong arming could ever be. He's offering a toe-to-toe battle with him, and that's the kind of threat the reckless part craves.

Because who knows where that kind of battle will end?

I'm thinking sweaty and naked.

"Why do you care, then?"

"I don't like being fucked over." His gaze slides slowly over me. "Fucked, on the other hand…"

I can't breathe as my stomach soars so high the room rocks around me. Finally, I get myself back under some semblance of control.

"I'm sure there are plenty of willing women begging to do that," I say.

"I'm sure there are."

I want to shake him for that smugness. Even though I taunted him into it. And he's right, we really are an interesting pair.

Shit. I focus back on the topic. One I need to tread carefully around, and one he's trying to throw me off balance and into the middle of. "I'm not out to stop you finding the tiara, Kingston. And I doubt your mother's going to go to those kind of dark lengths to do whatever it is you think she's doing."

"You think she's doing something, too."

"I asked a question," I say.

"One that didn't just appear from the ether."

"It stands to reason to question everything and everyone. Your mother, Jenson, the postman. I don't know, Kingston. I'm here trying to find something someone doesn't want found. And that can be hard when it comes to stolen goods like this. When it appears, we can make a move. We being me."

"We being we, you mean."

I breathe out and toss down the rest of my drink. Then I get up, and he hands me his glass. I shoot him a dirty look as I snatch it, and refill the glasses, deliberately giving him some white Spanish sherry.

He laughs when he takes a sip. "Nice try there, Sadie, but this is quality stuff."

"Asshole."

"So you've said."

I sit down and he slides closer, his arm on the back of the sofa. But he doesn't make a move to touch me and I'm not sure whether I'm relieved, annoyed, or suspicious. So I settle on all three.

"You think it'll turn up?"

"I don't think last night was any kind of happy coincidence. So yes, I think something will happen. I'm just trying to get a jump on it." And no one's talking. Not even Damon's heard anything, and he keeps his ear to the ground as a way to protect his clients. "An exceptionally expensive tiara is missing, but no one has gone to the police."

"They might not be announcing it."

"These things are recorded, there's protocol. The book that must be followed," I say. My tone's joking, but I'm not and he knows it. "What if it isn't real? What if the tiara isn't worth much?"

"It has to be," he says. "And when I get it back, I'm having it evaluated. Then you sell it. For me."

"You don't want it for the history or family meaning?"

"I've lived without it for almost thirty-six years, why should it matter?" He slides a little closer, setting his drink down on the side table, then focuses on me. "And why should it matter to you?"

"You're thinking it matters to me because I want it for myself." His expression doesn't change. "You might be right. I like beautiful things. I like expensive things."

He nods, but he's still considering me. "You don't live surrounded by riches, Sadie."

"I know. But you're not going to believe me if I say I want to help. Or I want to do this for the challenge."

Kingston smiles and smooths a strand of hair from my face. "No, but my opinion shouldn't matter. I think you do want it, but you don't know what you're going to do. And I'm not sure of the motivation behind that want."

"You don't know me."

"I know enough, Sadie. I know you're going to help me and then try and do whatever it is you're thinking of doing."

My hand clenches on my thigh. We're too similar, out for the money. But this tiara is part of his family history, a legacy, and as someone who doesn't have one—not if you don't count my father's deplorable ways—it saddens me. Angers me. And he deserves me stealing it out from under him.

I haven't done that before. Worked for people and stolen, but hey, there's always a first time.

He slides his fingers down my cheek to rest under my chin. His touch is warm fire, and it burns soft down into me. "Don't think you can steal from me, Sadie."

"If I did, you wouldn't notice."

"I notice everything about you."

I shiver and try to shift away, but there's something in his gaze that pins me to this spot. "You want to cash it in. I thought you loved your family."

He drops his hand but doesn't move from me, keeping that closeness, and the something in his eyes turns up to eleven. It's cold, dark fire that could combust into heat at any second. It's dangerous and addictive and I wouldn't move if someone paid me to.

"I do. I don't give a shit about the rest of it. If there's a legacy. What I care about is what it can bring me. I want the tiara and you're going to sell it to the highest bidder."

I shouldn't care. I know that.

"So, you really want to go through all this just to sell it?"

He smiles. "It's mine to do with what I want."

"You have to get it first."

"That's why I have you."

"You're a cold, money-focused bastard," I say deliberately.

His smile, already deadly, turns feral in all the right ways. "And you, my beautiful Sadie, are a common thief."

The air between us crackles like lightning.

I can't breathe. I can't think.

All there is, is him.

And then he moves, slow and deliberate, giving me all the time in the world to speak, to run.

I stay exactly where I am.

Everything in me is humming and buzzing and alive with a deep, dark need.

"Sadie…" He takes my glass and places it on the table in front of us. His gaze doesn't lift from mine.

And I'm so fucking alive I can barely breathe.

Kingston's mouth comes down on mine.

Chapter Seventeen

### *Kingston*

I kiss her because I want to. Because I have to. She's a fever, a need, and she's there.

This thing between us burns hotter than the sun, and continuously shoving it on some kind of backburner doesn't work.

Sadie tastes divine.

Her mouth opens beneath mine and I slide down into her. She's hot and wet and willing and I pull her to me as she wraps around me.

The need doesn't dissipate, it grows and there are too many clothes.

The kiss morphs into carnal hunger and we're at each other, pulling and touching until clothes go flying. I need her. Any way I can get her. I'm hard. Harder than I've ever been in my life and I don't think I've ever wanted anyone as much as Sadie.

She's in her bra, a lacy black number that clings to those soft, sweet mounds and I push my hand in her short hair, grasping, pulling her into me for a hungry kiss, one she takes and runs with.

Her hands slide over me, to my belt and she sits up, breaking the kiss and she looks at me, eyes molten rivers, and the look she gives shoots down to my gut, and my cock throbs. She's at the fly of my trousers and I help her. We're both in each other's way, consumed with the need for the other.

I pull at her jeans and she gets up and peels them off and then she's on me, hot and lithe, her mouth seeking mine. I need her. It's like air itself, that need. A beat and throb of such power I'm helpless to do anything but free myself to her hot hand, and she wraps about my thickness, my length, and begins to give me a hand job and she's lucky I don't come then and there.

She straddles me, her lace-clad pussy hovering above where she's working me and I want every part of her exposed. I want to explore her mouth again, her breasts, but fuck, I really want that hot little cunt.

I slide my hand down, fingers curling, down between her thighs, pushing up both sides of her, moving along the soft, wet heat of her outer lips and she hisses out air, pushing her hips, her pussy to my fingers.

Obliging her wordless request, we look at each other as I slip a finger, then two, beneath the lacy edge of her panties and then up into her.

Sadie cries out, biting her lip and she half closes her eyes, riding my fingers, grinding down into me and she shatters, coming hard and fast, the clench of her muscles on my fingers pushing me right to the edge.

I pull out my fingers and sweep the fabric to the side, and with my other hand, I pull hers away from me and then I pull her down and I push up, right into that hot, tight center of her.

"Oh, fuck, yes..." She moans the words and her hands come to my shoulders as she begins to ride me in earnest. I let her, because those fucking breasts are right there, and I want my mouth on them. I rip the fabric away, not caring if I actually ruin it—I'll buy her more. I'll buy her a fucking store full if I can ruin them all while she wears them.

Her breasts are gorgeous. Soft and round, the nipples a dark pink and I suck one into my mouth, biting down as it forms a peak on my tongue and she cries out, fingers digging into my nape.

"More."

I give her more. I want to fuck myself into her, so deep that no one else would ever dare touch her for fear of retribution. And then I lift my head and pull her down, and I take her mouth and I kiss her hard and deep and we fuck like that.

I need...I need more. I take hold of her and start working her on me and she's with me, moving hard, making little sounds that fuel me. She's the hottest thing I've seen, I've felt, and I need to mark her, claim her. It's a reflexive thing, wanting that. Primal, and I bite her neck, suckling.

Sadie comes again, her convulsions setting me off, pushing me right into release and the orgasm that rips through me is a wild, feral thing, and my vision goes black as the sweet burst of intense pleasure floods me to the point I don't know if I can survive it.

But finally, when the world comes to right, we stay there, her on me, slumped against me and... And I want to say that won't happen again, but I can't because I'm already thinking of fucking her again.

I'm trying to find the words to say. Me, a man who commands a company with a cool few billion, can't find words.

How can one woman do that to me? A woman I don't like?

I like her.

I like her a lot.

Sadie gets off me and starts to dress, but I take her arm. "Where's the bathroom?"

"You know where it is." I pull her back to me and she tumbles down into my arms and I turn so we're lying on the sofa together, a tangle of limbs. "You've been through my entire place and we both know it."

"Kingston..."

"You want me to let you go? I will." Those words are harder to say than they have any right to be. Because I don't want to let her go.

She sighs, her breath warm against me and I shiver. We're both half-dressed, ridiculously disheveled, and I don't want to let her go. I want to do it all over again. "What did we just do?"

I should laugh, but I don't. I can't. "I have no fucking idea, Sadie."

"That was a bad idea."

"The worst."

"I don't even like you, Kingston."

This time I slide her hair away from her face and smile. "I thought the same thing. About you. But then I realized that's a lie. And you're lying, too."

"Are you trying to tell me you're in love?"

"No. I don't believe in love. I like you and you like me."

"I liked that."

"Yeah." I close my eyes a moment and the thump-thump of her heart is oddly soothing. "That's putting it mildly."

"I don't regret it," she says, trailing her fingers down my shirt she ruined. "A one time only deal—"

"This isn't one time only. One night."

"One night."

We stare at each other and that beat is still in the air, that awareness and my cock stirs. Sadie shifts, very deliberately, against me.

"You play dangerously," I say to her.

She smiles. "I know." Then her smile fades. "We'd never last."

She's right there. We're not for each other, even though that might have been the best sex in my life. "Sadie, I..." I stop, unsure what it is I want to say. "I want to say that came from nowhere, or we were drunk, but it's not true. It's been brewing. And I'm sober."

"You and I don't work. We're too alike. We're too different. We...this is just weird."

Suddenly, I laugh and kiss her. It's a slow, lazy kiss, one that doesn't need to go anywhere, one that's warm and inviting and full of gentle waves of pleasure. It could go places, if we wanted it to. If one of us was to shift or turn it up a notch. But she doesn't do that and I lose myself in the sweetness of her mouth. The heat. The beauty of it. When I lift my head, I don't want to laugh anymore.

Because everything she said is why it would never work, even if by some weird turn of events we wanted it to. "Why are we talking about it?"

"Because I like to analyze, and so do you."

"This sofa is too fucking small," I say, getting up and stripping down.

Sadie watches, eyes bright with hunger. I reach out, take her hand and draw her to her feet and start stripping her, too.

"I can do that myself." But she doesn't try to stop me.

I glance up at her as I kneel down, pulling her panties off, the final article of clothing. The definite article, if you will. She's waxed bare, like she's been waiting for me. It's an incredibly erotic sight, her so exposed. And she's damp from our sex, her lips swollen, the skin a little reddened from that ride straight to heaven.

Before I can think about it, I take hold of her hips and put my mouth there, sliding my tongue down over her clit, and she rewards me with a sharp intake of breath, her body quivering.

"Part your thighs, Sadie."

She does.

I keep going. Sliding low, tracing my tongue along her slit, slipping into her, tasting the two of us, and the musk that's her.

Sadie groans low. I tongue fuck her, down and up, always coming to her clit to tease, a steady beat of movements until she's panting. Until she's wetter than before. Until she's pushing into my face. Her fingers are grasping at me and she's chanting yes.

I stop, and rise. Her face is flushed and she's shooting pure murder at me.

I drop a kiss on her mouth. "I think we should take this somewhere more comfortable."

And because I want to, because I can, I pick her up and she wraps about me and I take her to my bedroom.

"Asshole," she says.

In my room I drop her on the king bed and she looks good on the sea of navy and gray, splayed, open, inviting me in. She rises on her elbows, parting her legs wider for me and giving me that look that both dares me and tells me to go fuck myself, that look I know, that look which gets me hot.

Only this time, it's saying fuck you and fuck me and I'm very much into the latter when that invite comes from Sadie Hess.

I go down, making my way up her sweet body, kissing and tasting, nipping her inner thighs, just above her clit, deliberately missing all those delicious parts that make her shake apart because I really am an asshole and I want to tease her into a mindless state, one where she can't think, only feel.

Up I go, sucking a spot on her hip, biting her stomach, kissing her breasts, her throat, her shoulder, and then I take her mouth as I push into her.

This time we take it slow, a measured fuck that's erotic, a test in patience, one we both lose as that urgency comes over me. Her, too, from the way she moans and pulls at me, how she pushes up to meet each thrust, how her hands bite at me, like she's trying to get me further into her, and I want that.

It's no longer a game. It's a wordless merge, one of wild storms and high seas of need and pleasure that hovers, drawing me in. She's tight, so tight. And hot. Her slickness takes me each time I pound into her and her sharp little gasps of air a symphony just for me.

I want to lose myself in her, so far I come out the other side, born and free of her.

And as she shatters around me, dragging me into that release, I don't think I am.

Not at all.

# Chapter Seventeen

## KINGSTON

I kiss her because I want to. Because I have to. She's a fever, a need, and she's there.

This thing between us burns hotter than the sun, and continuously shoving it on some kind of backburner doesn't work.

Sadie tastes divine.

Her mouth opens beneath mine and I slide down into her. She's hot and wet and willing and I pull her to me as she wraps around me.

The need doesn't dissipate, it grows and there are too many clothes.

The kiss morphs into carnal hunger and we're at each other, pulling and touching until clothes go flying. I need her. Any way I can get her. I'm hard. Harder than I've ever been in my life and I don't think I've ever wanted anyone as much as Sadie.

She's in her bra, a lacy black number that clings to those soft, sweet mounds and I push my hand in her short hair, grasping, pulling her into me for a hungry kiss, one she takes and runs with.

Her hands slide over me, to my belt and she sits up, breaking the kiss and she looks at me, eyes molten rivers, and the look she gives shoots down to my gut, and my cock throbs. She's at the fly of my trousers and I help her. We're both in each other's way, consumed with the need for the other.

I pull at her jeans and she gets up and peels them off and then she's on me, hot and lithe, her mouth seeking mine. I need her. It's like air itself, that need. A beat and throb of such power I'm helpless to do anything but free myself to her hot hand, and she wraps about my thickness, my length, and begins to give me a hand job and she's lucky I don't come then and there.

She straddles me, her lace-clad pussy hovering above where she's working me and I want every part of her exposed. I want to explore her mouth again, her breasts, but fuck, I really want that hot little cunt.

I slide my hand down, fingers curling, down between her thighs, pushing up both sides of her, moving along the soft, wet heat of her outer lips and she hisses out air, pushing her hips, her pussy to my fingers.

Obliging her wordless request, we look at each other as I slip a finger, then two, beneath the lacy edge of her panties and then up into her.

Sadie cries out, biting her lip and she half closes her eyes, riding my fingers, grinding down into me and she shatters, coming hard and fast, the clench of her muscles on my fingers pushing me right to the edge.

I pull out my fingers and sweep the fabric to the side, and with my other hand, I pull hers away from me and then I pull her down and I push up, right into that hot, tight center of her.

"Oh, fuck, yes…" She moans the words and her hands come to my shoulders as she begins to ride me in earnest. I let her, because those fucking breasts are right there, and I want my mouth on them. I rip the fabric away, not caring if I actually ruin it—I'll buy her more. I'll buy her a fucking store full if I can ruin them all while she wears them.

Her breasts are gorgeous. Soft and round, the nipples a dark pink and I suck one into my mouth, biting down as it forms a peak on my tongue and she cries out, fingers digging into my nape.

"More."

I give her more. I want to fuck myself into her, so deep that no one else would ever dare touch her for fear of retribution. And then I lift my head and pull her down, and I take her mouth and I kiss her hard and deep and we fuck like that.

I need…I need more. I take hold of her and start working her on me and she's with me, moving hard, making little sounds that fuel me. She's the hottest thing I've seen, I've felt, and I need to mark her, claim her. It's a reflexive thing, wanting that. Primal, and I bite her neck, suckling.

Sadie comes again, her convulsions setting me off, pushing me right into release and the orgasm that rips through me is a wild, feral thing, and my vision goes black as the sweet burst of intense pleasure floods me to the point I don't know if I can survive it.

But finally, when the world comes to right, we stay there, her on me, slumped against me and… And I want to say that won't happen again, but I can't because I'm already thinking of fucking her again.

I'm trying to find the words to say. Me, a man who commands a company with a cool few billion, can't find words.

How can one woman do that to me? A woman I don't like?

I like her.

I like her a lot.

Sadie gets off me and starts to dress, but I take her arm. "Where's the bathroom?"

"You know where it is." I pull her back to me and she tumbles down into my arms and I turn so we're lying on the sofa together, a tangle of limbs. "You've been through my entire place and we both know it."

"Kingston…"

"You want me to let you go? I will." Those words are harder to say than they have any right to be. Because I don't want to let her go.

She sighs, her breath warm against me and I shiver. We're both half-dressed, ridiculously disheveled, and I don't want to let her go. I want to do it all over again. "What did we just do?"

I should laugh, but I don't. I can't. "I have no fucking idea, Sadie."

"That was a bad idea."

"The worst."

"I don't even like you, Kingston."

This time I slide her hair away from her face and smile. "I thought the same thing. About you. But then I realized that's a lie. And you're lying, too."

"Are you trying to tell me you're in love?"

"No. I don't believe in love. I like you and you like me."

"I liked that."

"Yeah." I close my eyes a moment and the thump-thump of her heart is oddly soothing. "That's putting it mildly."

"I don't regret it," she says, trailing her fingers down my shirt she ruined. "A one time only deal—"

"This isn't one time only. One night."

"One night."

We stare at each other and that beat is still in the air, that awareness and my cock stirs. Sadie shifts, very deliberately, against me.

"You play dangerously," I say to her.

She smiles. "I know." Then her smile fades. "We'd never last."

She's right there. We're not for each other, even though that might have been the best sex in my life. "Sadie, I..." I stop, unsure what it is I want to say. "I want to say that came from nowhere, or we were drunk, but it's not true. It's been brewing. And I'm sober."

"You and I don't work. We're too alike. We're too different. We...this is just weird."

Suddenly, I laugh and kiss her. It's a slow, lazy kiss, one that doesn't need to go anywhere, one that's warm and inviting and full of gentle waves of pleasure. It could go places, if we wanted it to. If one of us was to shift or turn it up a notch. But she doesn't do that and I lose myself in the sweetness of her mouth. The heat. The beauty of it. When I lift my head, I don't want to laugh anymore.

Because everything she said is why it would never work, even if by some weird turn of events we wanted it to. "Why are we talking about it?"

"Because I like to analyze, and so do you."

"This sofa is too fucking small," I say, getting up and stripping down.

Sadie watches, eyes bright with hunger. I reach out, take her hand and draw her to her feet and start stripping her, too.

"I can do that myself." But she doesn't try to stop me.

I glance up at her as I kneel down, pulling her panties off, the final article of clothing. The definite article, if you will. She's waxed bare, like she's been waiting for me. It's an incredibly erotic sight, her so exposed. And she's damp from our sex, her lips swollen, the skin a little reddened from that ride straight to heaven.

Before I can think about it, I take hold of her hips and put my mouth there, sliding my tongue down over her clit, and she rewards me with a sharp intake of breath, her body quivering.

"Part your thighs, Sadie."

She does.

I keep going. Sliding low, tracing my tongue along her slit, slipping into her, tasting the two of us, and the musk that's her.

Sadie groans low. I tongue fuck her, down and up, always coming to her clit to tease, a steady beat of movements until she's panting. Until she's wetter than before. Until she's pushing into my face. Her fingers are grasping at me and she's chanting yes.

I stop, and rise. Her face is flushed and she's shooting pure murder at me.

I drop a kiss on her mouth. "I think we should take this somewhere more comfortable."

And because I want to, because I can, I pick her up and she wraps about me and I take her to my bedroom.

"Asshole," she says.

In my room I drop her on the king bed and she looks good on the sea of navy and gray, splayed, open, inviting me in. She rises on her elbows, parting her legs wider for me and giving me that look that both dares me and tells me to go fuck myself, that look I know, that look which gets me hot.

Only this time, it's saying fuck you and fuck me and I'm very much into the latter when that invite comes from Sadie Hess.

I go down, making my way up her sweet body, kissing and tasting, nipping her inner thighs, just above her clit, deliberately missing all those delicious parts that make her shake apart because I really am an asshole and I want to tease her into a mindless state, one where she can't think, only feel.

Up I go, sucking a spot on her hip, biting her stomach, kissing her breasts, her throat, her shoulder, and then I take her mouth as I push into her.

This time we take it slow, a measured fuck that's erotic, a test in patience, one we both lose as that urgency comes over me. Her, too, from the way she moans and pulls at me, how she pushes up to meet each thrust, how her hands bite at me, like she's trying to get me further into her, and I want that.

It's no longer a game. It's a wordless merge, one of wild storms and high seas of need and pleasure that hovers, drawing me in. She's tight, so tight. And hot. Her slickness takes me each time I pound into her and her sharp little gasps of air a symphony just for me.

I want to lose myself in her, so far I come out the other side, born and free of her.

And as she shatters around me, dragging me into that release, I don't think I am.

Not at all.

# Chapter Eighteen

## SADIE

I t's late and I don't know how many times we've fucked. More than we should. Not nearly enough.

How this happened is both a mystery and completely inevitable. One night only, I tell myself. One night of insane pleasure that will keep me warm for winters to come.

Oh, how I'd love to say this was mediocre, but there's only so much lying I can do before it enters a ridiculous fantasy realm.

His arm is around me, heavy on my middle, and it feels good, right. It shouldn't.

Nothing about Kingston should.

It's not near dawn yet, but it's insanely late because we started so early. A part of me wishes I could go back in time, a very small part. The rest of me? Not on your fucking life would I trade sleeping with Kingston for anything. It has nothing to do with who and what he is on paper and everything to do with pure, old-fashioned chemistry.

I could curl up and sleep in his arms. I could spend a lifetime of him touching me gently, of him kissing me. Of sparring with his cynical bastard self, of cupping my hands around his rare sweet and naked smile, the one I've seen only hints of.

Like before we slept.

I go to lift his arm, but he shifts, pulling me in tighter and his thick length grows as he thrusts against me in slow, lazy moves.

A moan escapes. I'm that good kind of sore. That sweet ache that leaves an emptiness that yearns to be filled again, that only comes from phenomenal sex.

I know, because this...this is phenomenal sex with him. I've had great sex, but never this. Never the kind of mind melting thing that happens between us.

Reaching behind me, I wrap my hand around his beautiful cock and he groans, biting my ear. "Again?"

"Yes."

Once more and never again. It has to be that.

He's thrusting into my hand, slipping down to find the wetness between my thighs, sliding along my opening, dipping in only to come up to tease my clit that's aching for him, a bundle of live wires that suddenly need his touch to truly sing.

Kingston bites down on my throat and he starts to turn me on my back, but if I face him I might lose myself forever, so I roll the other way as I release him and push up to my hands and knees.

He doesn't need telling.

His hands come down on my hips and he uses his thigh to push my legs apart, and then he rubs himself against me. Dear God, this man can tease a woman to commit all kinds of crimes.

Letting go of my left hip, he lightly scrapes his short nails down my spine to my nape and he grips, pushing me down so my head is on the pillow and my ass is there for him.

He thrusts into me, deep. And my pussy stretches around that invasion.

It's so good a tremor of pleasure washes through me.

And then he starts to take me in slow, deep strokes. He's in total control and it's even hotter than it was before.

He pulls out and thrusts in. Long. Full. A slow kind of pounding that builds and builds, stretching my sanity, my absolute need for release to the very edge.

And then he lets go. Hard. That good kind of pleasure that vibrates right down to the marrow and I come. I come so hard I cry and then he wraps about me, moaning, coming down on me as he slams into me, over and over and he bites down on my shoulder as he comes, convulsing.

Finally, finally, we're done.

We have to be.

Otherwise I'm lost.

The sun is coming in gray when I finally sneak out. If I didn't think a man like Kingston would bring up what happened, I'd pretend it didn't happen.

But I can't.

As much as I hate myself for it, I don't want to, either.

I take a cab home because the last thing I want is the subway ride of shame. Not that I'm shamed. I just don't want to deal with looking like yesterday when everyone else is starting their today.

Besides, the sooner I'm home, the sooner I can get stuck into work and the sooner Kingston will be out of my life.

And maybe, just maybe, I'll take the tiara and whatever else as a souvenir.

Three hours later and I'm exhausted. More exhausted than I'd be if I'd been pounding the pavement hard.

And I really shouldn't think of the word pounding, as it takes my mind to other activities that could lead to exhaustion. The good kind. The naked, sweaty, depleted kind.

I lean back in my chair and stare at my laptop. It's not quite dark web that I'm trawling, but it's through a VPN, and for what I'm looking for I don't want to go too deep. I need to be where any action might be, in regards to the movement of the tiara.

Me taking the damn thing aside—if I choose to do that—I know I'm on to something about his mom. The whole missing jewel situation doesn't smell right. I don't care about police involvement. There are plenty of circumstances where above board things go around official channels.

But the timing...

That's what's bothering me.

The final jewel, rumored to be the most intricate, the one worth the most and certainly the one lusted after by collectors, not only appears along with the other Sinclair jewels, but it goes missing in time to fit in to the month before Kingston's birthday? And to get his slice of the family pie he has to make it appear again?

My involvement with his mother also has me suspicious.

Yes, she'd choose me or someone like me, but she seemed very keen I try and work with him. If he hadn't hired me himself, would she have thrown me into his path?

If so, for what reason?

I make a mental note of everything.

Well, I need to do something as all my leads and avenues I've followed have ended in exactly the same place—nowhere at all.

Sure, there are whispers and rumors that grow stronger, but that's all they are. People want it, no one is claiming to have it.

But instinct tells me they will. And soon.

Whether that soon will be in time for Kingston's deadline, I don't know.

It depends on who has it. And if it was actually stolen.

I'm waiting for Damon to get back to me when he bangs on my door. It has to be Damon because he knows how to get into places and I made sure the security to this building is top notch.

I get up and stomp to the door, throwing it open. "Damon..."

It's most definitely not Damon. I look up to the unsmiling face of the dark lord himself, Kingston Sinclair.

I don't know why an inexplicable warmth rushes my veins.

"Is that his name?"

"Who?" I glare at him.

He glares back. "The mythical ex."

Kingston pushes past me and into my apartment that suddenly feels too small.

"One." I tick these off on my hand. "He's not mythical. Two, I've said his name before. Three, at least I mentioned I have an ex and you're all into keeping women like deep, dark secrets. Four, what the hell business is it of yours? And five...are you jealous?"

"Don't be ridiculous. I'm not looking for a relationship, so why would I be jealous?"

I shove my hands on my hips. "I don't know. You called him my mythical ex."

"He's back to being a boyfriend now? You move fast." Kingston goes to my computer, looking at the screen. "And I don't keep them like deep, dark secrets. I keep them labeled, in boxes on a shelf, for ease."

"You're—"

"An ass?"

"What do you want, Kingston?" He's drawing me in with his weird charm and I don't want to be drawn in, or charmed.

Maybe I'll steal everything from him. It would serve him right.

"What's this?" He thumbs at the computer.

"Work."

"For me?"

I breathe out. What was that about charm? "Yes. I put everything on hold for this."

"And?"

"If you're asking why I'd do that, I don't know and I'm regretting life choices," I say. "If you're asking about the tiara, I don't have anything."

He looks at me long and hard. "Unless you're hiding something."

"If I was hiding something from you, then you would never know."

We're a rollercoaster of unspoken things. Up and down and all over the place at breakneck speed and I can pinpoint the exact moment we got on board. It was when he kissed me last night.

I really am going to steal everything from him. Duante comes to mind, but I'll deal with him when I get my hands on the jewel and not before. Instead, I fold my arms. "You can relax. Last night was sex and nothing more. Don't get your panties in a twist."

"I prefer to wear high cut non-twistable panties, like all the big boys," he says in a low and dangerous voice, "and I'm not here about that. I don't give a flying fuck about that. Sex is sex, Sadie. Right? We decided that. So, pull up your big girl boxers and get it together. If you want a repeat, just ask. I'll pencil you in."

He's angry. Deeply, darkly angry and I can't work out why. He knows where we are with all this tiara business. I haven't had time to find and steal the damn thing. And he doesn't care about the sex beyond it being sex—the pang inside is something I ignore—so whatever his problem is, he better get it out in the open or when things happen he's going to fuck it up for himself.

Things like losing the tiara. That is, of course, if I don't steal it to teach the idiot a lesson.

"You're going to have to tell me why you're so furious, Kingston."

He pushes a hand through his hair. "Because I'm not sure I trust you."

"In what way?"

"In the maybe you have the tiara way."

"I don't." I breathe out. It's time to put my own petty little fantasies to one side and play big ball. "I won't be able to make money from it if I have it."

"You will if you double bluff me to push up the price for me to get it back in time."

Actually, I never thought of that. Because I might still keep a hand in the water, but I don't ever drink that water. I haven't stolen in years, just like I'm sure I told him when we met.

And sure, I've been currently entertaining the idea of taking it all for me if I can, but that's just entertaining an idea, not doing. Not following through.

"I'm not going to do that. I have a reputation here. One you know is built on a weird trust. If it gets out I stole it, if you spread that rumor, then I'm done in my line."

"Well, I—" He stops. "Okay. I might be angry. Frustrated, I guess is the word. But time is running out, Sadie, and we're exactly nowhere. What am I meant to think?"

"That the world doesn't work on your whim. And we're not nowhere. I'm looking, I'm following all sorts of leads. So far, it's just rumor and whispers, but something is going to happen. I feel that."

"And if it doesn't?"

"Then I'm wrong."

I might hate him, I realize, for his complete lack of trust in me. I don't care if it's warranted or not. I haven't actually done anything to him. Yet.

"So if you're wrong, we don't find it? Is that what you're telling me?"

"That's not an option," I say. "Because that option means I lose. And that's one thing I don't do."

# Chapter Nineteen

## KINGSTON

T he expression on her face kills me.

I burst in here—jealous as fuck when she called out the name Damon in the kind of voice that told me way too much—and got in her face and then I tell her I don't trust her.

I'm a complete asshole.

What I should be is happy she left. Happy she's not trying to entwine our lives together. I don't want that. She doesn't either, so why I'm so angry I don't get. But I am.

The fierceness of her tone doesn't match the naked vulnerability in her eyes, her expression.

Because she's right, I could put an end to her sweet little career of catering to the rich by evaluating their security.

And the trust thing? Yeah, I don't know if I do trust her with the tiara, but I trusted her enough to get down and dirty with in so many filthy and delightful ways I still ache. My cock twitches at the memories and the pleasure she can bring.

Like when she went down on me at some hour between time four and six. This isn't helping me here, so I put the sex to one side. As much as I can because damn, I could take her now.

"Trust me or don't trust me," she says, "but I'm not going to lose. We'll work out something."

Suddenly, I laugh and shake my head. "In another world, we'd be perfect for each other. We're way too alike. Neither one likes losing and we'll both do what it takes. And you know what, in that I do trust you. But..."

There's something about her. She's being ballsy, way more than usual and I don't know if it's because she has something planned she's not telling me about, or whether it's over last night and at this point, as long as my end result works in my favor, I don't care.

I don't want to wait. I need this to be over. Because something tells me the longer she's in my life, the deeper she'll go and the harder it'll be to forget her.

And that's already going to be near impossible.

"But what?" She casts me a look then goes over to shut her computer down, deliberately. In exaggerated moves, to show me she didn't like me snooping. Well, too fucking bad.

"But we're never having a relationship."

Sadie looks up, pausing, a notebook in hand. And she laughs. It's the kind of laugh that makes heat flare and burn up the back of my neck and to my face. "A...relationship? You think I want a relationship? With you?"

"No." I keep my expression neutral. "But I'm putting it out there. I don't usually go around—"

"Fucking criminals?"

"Fucking women without an understanding."

Sadie dumps the notebook and comes over, and pats my arm. Hard. "Relax there, hot man. Because you're hot. But hot doesn't mean I want to subscribe to Picket Fences Monthly. We had great sex, Kingston. I've had great sex before. And I didn't send out cards announcing we're going steady. I'm not about to do that with you, either." She pauses. "Especially when it comes to you."

"Good. Great. We're on the same page."

"To the word."

I'm not happy, though. Sure, I'm relieved she doesn't think there's more, but nothing about this makes me happy. Not one single thing. The sooner she's out of my life, the better. Call that my mantra of the current times.

"We need a plan," I finally say.

"For what? I told you, I don't want to be with you. Sure, you're rich, hot, gorgeous. You tick a lot of boxes for a lucky lady out there. I'm not her. I don't want to be her."

She doesn't quite look at me as she says this and she turns back to her desk, continuing to close books and notebooks and tidy up.

I breathe out. I don't know why, but I can't shake the feeling I've fucked things up.

"I'm talking about a plan for the tiara. I think we should push, see what happens."

Sadie turns to face me and gives me a curious look. "We have one. And right now we don't have a castle to storm."

I go back to my damn mother. I'm positive Sadie's been employed by her, thrown my way, or would have been if I hadn't found her first. But while I'd love to know the truth, again it comes to me it doesn't matter. Unless, of course, my mother is out to... What? Actually destroy the company?

No, it's not that.

While I keep going back to that, over and over again, just like I do with her involvement with Sadie, Mother's not going to hurt me. Nor my brothers. And Sadie...yeah, as much as I like to know everything, that ultimate truth isn't important, either.

Still.

I lean against the sofa's back in Sadie's living room, the gray light outside making the colors in here brighter. "You asked me a question about my mother."

"We talked about that."

"I know." I put my hands to either side of me and clench my fingers into the firm and thick top of the sofa's back. Like it's going to stop me from going to Sadie. "I keep coming back to it."

"You and your mommy issues aren't mine."

I grin. There's the Sadie I like. All sharp-edged sass and snark. It soothes the soul. It riles. "She's not about to hurt me."

"She does know you," Sadie says.

I nod. "In spite of that."

She gives a short burst of laughter, then pulls her scowl back in place. "I'll overlook that fault."

"My mother's not about to hurt me, but I think I want to find out what Faye's involvement in all this is."

Sadie's scowl melts as excitement takes its place. "Are you thinking if she is involved she might know of the tiara's whereabouts?"

"It's worth a try."

She rubs a hand over her face and comes up to me. "What are you thinking?"

"I don't know. You're the criminal."

"Your diabolical, twisted mind gives mine a run for the money."

I laugh softly. "A test. You're telling me you think it'll turn up soon. There'll be some kind of event if we don't find it first?"

"Ye-es." She stares at me hard. "But I'm hoping to find the damn thing first."

"Why don't you put word out that you're on the trail or you have it? I don't know?"

"How will that work? I think we need more."

I straighten up now and step a little closer to her and if I breathe in her smoke and jasmine then it's just there, not because I crave that tiny taste of her. "Like what, Sadie?"

"You want to get word back to your mother—if she's deeply involved—and see what happens?"

"Exactly."

She nods. "Then we'll need more than to get word out and a fake trail full of nothing. We're currently surrounded by all of that bullshit, and that's the problem. Adding to it won't make a difference. If you want to test how deep your mother's involvement is, then we need a solid plan."

"I'm listening."

"You could ask her."

I snort. "She's even more diabolical than me. Maybe even more than you."

"Such sweet words, Kingston." She bites the corner of her lip a moment, then her gaze flies up to mine. "Photos."

"You want me to show her photos?"

She spins away and starts pacing, the air thickening with the excitement rolling off her. She's so fucking hot when she's like this.

What am I thinking?

Sadie is fucking hot all the time.

"Not a bad idea, but I mean, are there photos of the jewels now? More than the ones I've seen?"

"Jenson catalogs everything. Yes."

"Get them."

"Why?"

"A fake."

I stare at her. "A fake tiara? You want...how the hell do we do that? It's going to have to go to Jenson."

"If we get that far with it. I have a plan."

"And I'm all ears," I say. "What's the plan?"

"I just told you a fake. I'm going to get you a fake."

"Who do you know?" I ask.

She smiles.

And if I believed in love, this would be the exact moment I fell in love with Sadie.

If.

# Chapter Twenty

## SADIE

Kingston is leaning against my building's wall when I come out the next morning.

Little flurries of snow that melt the moment they touch anything make the early cold snap more fun.

He's a gorgeous sight all in black, tall, lean, austere beauty almost hypnotic. He's compelling, and that compulsion, that draw to him, is made even more addictive by the heavenly scent of rich coffee from the steaming requisite New York deli to-go cups.

Kingston's blue gaze punches me hard as it greets me and I struggle to breathe as he sips a cup in his left hand and holds forth the other in his right.

"Is this bodega coffee?"

"I felt like slumming it."

I laugh and take the cup. It isn't from a crap bodega. This is from one of the retro-style coffee places on Avenue C, barista made. I narrow my eyes from him after I take a sip.

"I lied," he says. "There are only so many sacrifices a man can make and good coffee isn't one of them."

"You're not being wheeled about on a golden platform, so there's hope for you."

I start walking. I don't look back or wait. Kingston Sinclair is there, easily keeping my pace as we power down the street in the early morning.

"I don't know when it became verbally beat up the billionaire week, but you keep upping the ante in your insults," he says with way too much cheer for seven-thirty a.m. "Is there a prize at the end of the week?"

"No. I'm just doing it for fun." And to cover the spot of pain that lurks dark and dank in my chest, right down deep where I can't get to it. "How did you know I'd be up early?"

He shrugs. "I just figured you were wanting to get a jump on the counterfeit. And I have your photos."

Kingston pulls a manilla envelope from his beautiful jacket that's probably yak silk. I don't know if there's such a thing, but if there is and it's rare and expensive, then he'll have it.

I'm being horrible and unfair, because he might have a thing for ridiculously expensive watches, but he's not anything like the people I usually work for, who love to show off through money. For someone like him, he's remarkably down to earth and I find that dangerous. To me.

"Thanks." I shove the envelope in my bag and swing it back onto my shoulder, managing not to spill or drop the coffee.

"You're welcome." We pause at the lights. "But I was going to ring your bell if you hadn't appeared."

I glance at him. "Not let yourself into the building like yesterday?"

"No, I like to keep the element of surprise."

An itch to ask starts, but I keep my mouth firmly shut, even as his twitches up in a smile.

"You want to ask, don't you, Sadie?" Kingston shakes his head, his breath little fleeting puffs of white. "Good to know."

"Did you just come to annoy me?"

"The photos?"

"Nope. You want more."

"Damn fucking right. I want to follow up on our conversation last night." The smile is gone as we continue walking toward the East Village.

I huff out a breath. "I told you I'll see what I can do."

"You're doing it today." This isn't a question and we both know it. "Time's getting shorter. I need this underway today or we have to hit the drawing board again. So, where are we off to?"

I'm off to see Athena. He—he can do whatever he damn well wants. I shove my free hand in my pocket and take a swallow of the cooling coffee. There's too little milk for my liking and no sugar, but I'm guessing this is how he sees me liking my brew—almost black and bitter.

Pretty apt, I guess.

"This is going to cost you. Because this needs to be good enough that it'll pull the wool over expert eyes. If it comes down to that."

He stops and I do, too.

"Explain, Sadie."

"If this is shown to Jenson and your mother and they call someone in, then we have to make it look like the real deal. The upside is if they don't have the real one, then the expert will have to go on what they know about the jeweler."

He frowns and someone yells at us for blocking the path. Kingston mutters something and takes my arm, leading me to the side near a building. "We're planning on going that far?"

"Prepare for all contingencies," I say. "And..." I suck in a breath, because this is something I spent hours thinking about, long after he left. "I don't like to lose, but I'm not above subterfuge."

"Sadie." He says my name as a warning, almost a question. He's a smart man, he's cottoning on to what I mean.

I shrug, aware he's still touching me and though my coat is warm enough, he turns my internal temperature up to high tropics, just from that touch of his hand on my arm.

"It might be the only way. If it is really missing and we can't get it, then we need plan B. This is it."

"We pass your fake off as the real deal to my mother and Jenson."

I nod.

His mouth is grim as he sighs. "Plant B is the last shot, Sadie. I'd prefer to do this above board if we can. Just for myself. But if not? Fuck it. We do that, we save the company with the fake, and then…"

"We part ways."

His eyes turn blazing. "Fuck no. We work together until I get that thing back. It's mine."

Yia-yia's head is bent down over the photos as she runs reverent fingers over the images. She hasn't said anything to me since she opened the folder at her worktable.

That suits me fine. Kingston is way too much in my head right now for me to carry on a meaningful conversation. And I know her well enough to leave her be while she's looking at a job.

He's not going to be happy. Minutes after he informed me he was coming with me—I think the words were "sticking to you like epoxy"—we hit Avenue A and first miracles of miracles, a yellow cab with a vacant sign headed towards us. I flagged it down and jumped in.

There's going to be words if I know him. But I need this time. And he's already invaded so much, I don't need him in every single aspect of my life.

It feels a little too intimate. Too pervasive. Too permanent.

And he's right. I'm not for him.

Could you imagine? A billionaire and an ex-criminal who can't shake her past? Not the past where I was the Raven, but the darker one, the fetid one, that part which is part of me, stretching back to when I landed in my father's care. If anyone can call it care.

If it hadn't been for Athena…

Suddenly I look over at the woman in question, the one who saved me. She's no longer studying the photos. She's studying me.

And I resist the urge to squirm.

"Well?"

"You know what I think, honey." She eyes me again and sighs, one bright blue fingernail stroking an image. "I want to know what you think."

"That you're not the sweet old lady everyone thinks you are."

Athena snorts and rises from the chintz chair. "Drop the old and we'll talk." But the humor doesn't reach her eyes. "Not about this. About the man tying you in knots."

"He's no one."

"Not many people would call a billionaire that. Then again, the mold was destroyed when you came along, Sadie."

"I don't want to talk about it." I don't. I do. I'm lost and I damn well know it. But soon he'll be gone and I can forget him. Or pretend to, anyway. Every word I said to him about us never being a thing and me not wanting it to be is true. Doesn't make the ache inside go away, though.

"I've known you were ten. I managed to get you away from him and we formed a good team, dodging the system, so I know you. And your tells. And honey, you're not even trying to hide anything right now."

"Because," I say, "there's nothing to hide. Nothing's going on."

"If you say so."

I glance at the pictures and then at her. "Can you do it?"

Yia-yia laughs. "I'm not an amateur. I'm the best."

She was also a master jeweler in her own right, but her real skill lay in counterfeit jobs and she knows it. "I'm not stroking your ego, Yia-yia."

"Of course I can. It'll cost."

"Clearly, he can pay."

She picks up a photo. "Remember when we met? You tried to fence me some piece of crap your father made you steal. I still have that."

"It was junk."

"Monetarily, yes. But not all things of value have a big dollar price tag." She looks from the photo and to me. "Do you understand what this is worth? Or, should I say, does your young man?"

"He's not my anything. Unless you mean a pain in my ass." I cross my arms. "Because he's that."

"There are worse things, Sadie."

Oh, God. She wants to talk in riddles and I don't have the time. "Kingston knows it's very expensive. And it's his. The real one. I'm going to get it back. He'll sell it, well, technically I will for him. That is, if I don't steal it, instead."

"Sadie!"

I roll my eyes. "I won't, but officially, I haven't decided."

"Hmmm, so you both think the price is the tag it would be given in a store?"

"Yes."

Athena spreads the photos out, moving them about in some kind of order that pleases her. "I thought I taught you better than that. You are better than that."

"I'm a thief."

"Ex. You did what you needed. Just like I did. We all do things to get by. But I honed all your skills and you took to that. You ran with it. You had your short-lived wild days, and you never hurt anyone. Never took from anyone who couldn't afford it."

"I don't regret it."

She meets my gaze with those eyes that see too much and I swallow. I do. I regret the stealing when I didn't have to, but I can't turn back the clock. I've managed to turn that into a way to stop others from doing the same with my clients. Christ, I should give myself a fucking parade for my virtue.

I'm pathetic.

I take a breath. Maudlin and regrets never help. Learning from mistakes does. This lady who is family to me taught me that. And I know she's trying to teach me something else.

"I know what you regret, Sadie, honey. But the past is the past. I gave you tools, but you're the one who got away from the life your father would have sucked you into. And I think without me, you'd have found your way. So don't let that color decisions now."

I frown. "I'm not."

"And be careful of playing games."

"I'm not doing that, either."

She smiles softly, like she can see things I can't. And it's annoying. "Be careful. Certain games bite back hard." Athena turns and sits. "Now, this job..."

"You can do it? A rush job?"

"I'm the best no one has heard of for a reason. Yes, I can do it."

I know it's been a while for her. But if I have faith in anyone it's Yia-yia, even if she's having a Confucius moment.

My phone beeps. I pull it from my pocket. Damon. "I need to go. I can leave this with you?"

"Yes." She waves me away with a hand, her head clearly already immersed in the job. "Remember what I said."

I murmur a yes and head out. I don't need to heed warnings. I'm fucking secure in my decisions.

She thinks I'm playing a game of the hearts with Kingston, but she couldn't be more wrong. We've laid everything on the table. Everything is clear as glass and lacking any tricky depths.

Sure, I might lust for him, but I don't really want him. He's too like me. Also, he's from a different world. He doesn't want me either, not beyond the sex.

And I can live with that.

Even if I like him more than I want to admit.

# Chapter Twenty-One

## KINGSTON

The last person I expected to see when I knocked was an old lady with improbable hair, neon blue nails, and an attitude that could rival Sadie's.

"I won't ask who you are," she says, not moving out of the way or extending an invitation.

Oh yeah, she's definitely linked to Sadie.

"So you're who she came to see." I don't move. I'm going in, and if I have to stand here all day, I will.

I'm not being an asshole, but I would like to know where my money is going. And why the fuck Sadie bolted from me.

This is, she might have gotten a cab, but so did I. There were two of them, and it was easy enough to flag the second down. I've even been known to use the subway before.

Her heavily lined and mascaraed eyes dip as she looks me over. "An actual billionaire on my humble doorstep."

"They'll be lining up soon."

She gives a bark of laughter. "If you want information, you'll have to ask your Raven."

"She's not my anything," I say, shoving my hands in my pockets, even though the hall of her building is warm. "But money is money."

The old lady sighs. "You sound like she said."

"An asshole?"

"Complex."

"I didn't say anything complex there, quite the opposite."

She smiles. "You did, you know. So did she." She looks me up and down. "Athena. And you look like the kind of man not about to go until he gets what he wants, so you might as well come in."

I follow her inside, and it's cozy. It's not the home of a thief. Then again, neither is Sadie's. Actually, what the fuck am I even thinking? How would I know? I don't hang around with criminals on any kind of basis.

A smile threatens to break free. Sadie would, of course, disagree with that. And she wouldn't be meaning her.

"I know you're looking for the Sinclair jewel."

"Me and everyone else, apparently," I say, sitting on the sofa because I'm towering over her and somehow, this short old lady with ridiculous nails and hair is making me feel small.

Like she's the one with power.

And maybe she is. Because Sadie came here. "You know where it is?"

"No one does, Mr. Sinclair," she says.

"That's not true. Someone does."

"That someone ain't Sadie."

I cross my legs and fold my hands and give her a cool look. "I don't know who you are, Athena."

The niceness falls away and her gaze turns hard. "Listen, bub," she says, heavy on the mocking tone, "You invited yourself here. You followed the person you hired."

"I don't trust her."

"You don't strike me as the kind of man who hires people he thinks might steal from him."

"Desperate times."

I look about the room. Everything is tasteful, but nothing worth more than it should for a place like this. Lived in, cared for, but not full of riches. The lamp on the table catches my eye, along with the photo propped up.

The tiara.

"What? You don't think a lady in her forties can recreate that?" She says this quietly and I swing my gaze back to her. She hasn't seen forty in decades, but I keep that to myself.

"I think you very probably can." I consider her. "Although the real thing would be better."

She snorts. "So you say. But we don't know where it is."

"Maybe Sadie's taken after her father."

The woman's face turns hard. "She has his talents, all right, but taking after him? Not on your pathetic pampered life."

I nod. "And how do I know that?"

"I don't care." She crosses her arms. "That girl had a hard life. But that's her story to tell—if she chooses. I will tell you this. She's smart and has honor and she managed to have the courage to walk away from a life she could have embraced and lived on easy street as they say."

"Sadie's a pain in my ass and probably the smartest, trickiest person I've met."

"So it's true love, then," she says.

The words are framed in sarcasm, but they hit me in the solar plexus with their quiet undertone, like she means it.

"Sorry, Athena. I don't believe in love. It's not part of my DNA."

She nods. "Break her heart and I'll break you. Just because I'm old doesn't mean I can't and it definitely doesn't mean I won't."

"Are you...are you threatening me?" I can't control the grin because as she nods, I like this woman. A lot.

"I believe I am making you a promise, Mr. Sinclair."

"Sadie gets her ballsiness from you, then."

"Hers is very much her own," Athena says. "And Sadie's tough, but there's softness if you look. She's also closed off, because she's vulnerable. She never had... She's worth it, if you give her a chance."

"It's a business relationship."

One of her brows rise. "So business put those hickeys on her neck, then?"

Heat rushes my face. How she just managed to embarrass me like a teenager is beyond me, but I let it slide, because she's looking at me like she's got my number.

"I thought so. Now, do you want to sit there making a damn fool of yourself, or do you want to learn how I create fakes, and maybe try and weasel some more information about Sadie from me?"

I smile. "Now, how can I resist such an offer? Lead the way. I'm all yours."

Athena didn't tell me anything about Sadie that I didn't know. Not in words. But there was a world in all the things she didn't say as well as the seemingly insignificant things.

Then there was the knock on the door, followed by a teen barreling in, wide-eyed, bloody nose. I'd been leaving, and the look she gave me told me to continue on my way.

But not before I got a glimpse of why the woman wasn't surrounded by riches—because she certainly could be judging by the work room and some of the things in there. They were old, the finished pieces, kept because she liked them. And when she slipped the kid money, and how she spoke to him, I knew she'd helped Sadie, too.

As I knock on my mother's door and wait, I can't keep it all out of my head.

The old reprobate clearly helped kids. And I'm betting a considerable chunk of my fortune that she uses her skills to make sure these kids and their families are looked after.

I'm betting she keeps kids out of broken systems and tries to bring them a better life.

Does everyone suddenly possess bleeding hearts?

"Kingston?"

I almost jump. "Sorry, it's been a long couple of weeks," I say to my mother.

Normally her housekeeper answers the door, but it must be the woman's day off.

"Come in."

I follow her through the great hall and into her sitting room. It's feminine with a modern edge, and not how we grew up. I look at her. She's pacing. "What are you up to?"

"I could ask you the same question, Kingston. Time is running out."

"Well, you and Jenson managed to somehow allow the final jewel to be stolen."

"No one allows such things." She pours tea into a porcelain cup and offers it to me.

I take it. The delicate cup and saucer with the tiny painted flowers and rim of gold looks ridiculous in my big hand. And I'm not fond of tea.

"What do the police say?"

"What I'd like to know," she says, stirring milk and sugar into her cup, "is what progress you've made."

"I did ask a question."

Her gaze skitters to me. "Time is running out. What are you going to do when you find it?"

"If. And it's not your business."

"It's a family heirloom."

"It's mine and something I'm going to be jumping through hoops to win." She sighs. "Kingston."

"What? You don't answer anything."

"It's been seen, you know. I have ears to the ground." She continues to look at me.

I set the teacup down. "What are you up to?"

"That's what I'm asking you."

"You could end this, and you know it."

"And how can I do that? Your father was of sound mind when he did all this." She blows on the steaming tea then takes a sip.

I narrow my eyes. "Yeah, but who put him up to it. You?"

This woman could win awards in evasion. And I continue to probe and she continues to calmly dodge until I've had enough.

"We need to stop these games, Mother."

"What games? I've heard your tiara has been seen, and I wanted to know if you'd gotten it back or had a plan." She smiles. "That's all."

"Yeah, right. Something bigger is going on and I want to know your part in it."

My mother sighs. "What do you mean?"

"You're keeping me from my piece of the Sinclair jewel collection." I pick my cup up and take a swallow, the tannins bitter and drying on my tongue. "I want to know what the big picture is here."

"It's gone, Kingston. You need to bring it back or the business is gone. That's the only picture."

"Now why don't I believe you?"

There's steel behind her calm and genteel smile. My mother is definitely up to something.

"Believe what you want, darling. It's all in your hands."

"You know, I'm going to sell it when I get it. Turn a profit."

There's a long silence. And finally, she asks, "Don't you think it might mean something?"

"I really don't care."

"Turn a profit. You think it's all about money. That worth."

"Of course I do. Money matters."

"Some things are worth more than money," she says, after another long beat. And she takes a swallow of her tea.

But I shake my head. "Money rules above all else."

"Really?"

"Yes, Mother. It's the only constant. It brings success and power and stability. Everything else can waver, but money only matters."

She sets down the cup and saucer. "And love, Kingston? Does that come with a monetary value, too?"

"Come on. You get it."

"Do I? I believe in love. I think it's important, Kingston. I think it's a constant. Steadier than money. And you don't?"

I just laugh. "No."

And it's true. Love doesn't exist.

# Chapter Twenty-Two

## SADIE

It's two days later and though I have leads, whoever has the tiara, whoever is trying to sell it, is laying low. But there's something in the air, something buzzing everywhere I look.

Something, somewhere in this underworld is going to happen and soon. People are excited.

I'd bet my life it's the Sinclair tiara.

Nothing gets the air sizzling like the discovery of a myth as reality. Especially in the world of the rare and unique and stolen.

But tonight I have different plans.

I stand in front of Kingston's door on his private landing. He's not expecting me, but here I am, ready to see the bastard who makes my heart beat a little too hard and fast.

Footsteps clatter and grow louder inside and I ring the bell again.

"I told you, I'm not in the mood." And the door swings open.

I forget how to breathe.

He doesn't move. "You're not my brother."

Oh, Lord, I don't know how, but this is somehow more naked than if he was naked.

Kingston's been working out, and he's wearing shorts that sit low on narrow hips, and sweat drips down from his hair and his pecs and I'm about to lose my mind.

All that man flesh, lean, the sheen and tiny rivulet of sweat is something I want to put my mouth against and lick off him. I've never had the inclination to lick sweat before, but with him?

Yes. Please.

My mouth is dry and words have vanished and my body throbs. Down deep between my thighs it thrums with the urge to have him touch, to slide his hands under my coat and throw me against the wall. I want him to slide fingers along my panties, I want them inside me. I want—

Fuck.

"Go shower and get dressed."

"And here I thought you were having a good old visual feast there." He steps aside, just a little, and I skitter in.

Kingston closes the door behind me and rests his hand against me, trapping me in. His body heat seeps down into me.

"You stink." He doesn't. The man smells faintly of that spice and musk of him, along with clean sweat, the kind that makes images of sex dance through my mind. As a way to get him to go away it's pathetic. And he knows it.

"If I do, it turns you on," he says, gaze on my mouth. He flicks open the buttons on my coat, pushing it open, though that's all he does. He slides his gaze over me. "Going somewhere?"

"With you, yes. Although, I want to kill you."

"See, that's why you're single, Sadie. You keep offing the men. Like a black widow spider."

"And your special blend of insulting women along with your personality is why you're single."

He moves in close. "If I kissed you, you'd kiss me back."

Before I can do a thing, he steps away and walks off. "Why are you here? Dressed to the nines?"

"We're going to your brother's fundraiser."

Christ, the lean, muscular shape of him is scorching even from behind.

I trail him down the hall and into the huge kitchen in white and black stone. He grabs a tea towel and wipes his face, flings it over his shoulders, around his neck. He then pours some water, sliding a glass to me and then getting one of his own. "I already donated."

"I don't care."

"Those things bore me."

They bore me, too, but he's going. We have a lot to talk about, like why he's keeping shit from me when I've been an open book about work. Things like visiting my Yia-yia.

She's no better, but Athena let it slip she's seen him, wrapping the reveal in the kind of words I'd have to basically say I was interested in him to get her to tell me more. Because Yia-yia is good.

The woman knows how to veil words without saying they'd spoken outright. It pisses me off.

"Why did you go to see Athena?"

His eyes widen slightly. "I'm betting she didn't tell you."

"Not in so many words."

Kingston shrugs and holds onto the ends of the towel that's lying around his neck. "Why do you think, Sadie?"

"Because you're an asshole."

He laughs and leans against the stone island. "Trust is delicate." He picks up his glass and takes a swallow.

"Or in your case, non-existent."

Kingston sighs. "You're not explaining why you think I'm going."

"Because it's invitation only."

"And since when has that stopped you?"

I consider him, then nod. "This is easier. And, it's your family."

"Okay, I'll bite. Why do you want to go to a fundraiser run by my brother? It's a small thing, big money. Not exactly a let's find the tiara event, is it?"

I could lie outright, tell him I suspect someone there might have a connection, but that's a dangerous game with him. Danger doesn't bother me when it's for a reason. Or when the person I'm playing with isn't a threat. This man is. To me. In dark, intimate ways.

He sees more than most.

There's tinder between us that's been doused in a combustible that's waiting for a match. It's been lit before, and it wants that again. I want it, even as much as I don't.

So I choose a half-truth. "Your mother will be there."

"You want her to see us together?"

"I want to see her in action."

Kingston smiles slowly. "You know that's flimsy."

He's right, it is, and I deliberately breathe evenly. "Let's just say I'm curious."

"Okay," he says after a small pause, "give me fifteen."

The party is in full swing when we get to the impressive loft in TriBeCa. His brother, Ryder, opens the door and old school jazz wraps about us.

The man is most definitely Kingston's brother, and he's probably the most stunning man I've met. He's hands-down, unobjectively beautiful.

But I prefer Kingston's beauty and its hard edge.

"Normally this is Mag's thing, but sometimes you gotta do your duty. And I thought you weren't coming, King," he says by way of greeting. Then his gaze lights on me and he grins. "Your taste has improved."

"If you're going to be doorman..." Kingston takes off his coat and hands it to his brother, who dumps it.

"Ryder." A tall redhead who reminds me of a film star from yesteryear approaches and collects the coat, hanging it up on a stand. There are staff, I can see them and no doubt there's a set up for coat check, but this is family and the party isn't huge. It's big enough and yet, not at all the kind of thing I'm expecting, though, taking in the man with the coal-black curls in his dark purple suit, it all fits.

These two are as different as I could have imagined, but it's clear they're brothers and not just from looks. There's steel beneath that layer of natural flirt and charm of Ryder, and his gaze smokes for the redhead. No jewels on her except a ring on her left hand.

Ryder slides a hand about her waist. "What? I'm allowed. He's my asshole brother."

"I'm not the only one who sees it," I say to Kingston.

He doesn't look insulted. "He projects. And you..."

"Me?"

"Have other reasons."

He's got me there. Kingston is an asshole, but his words have an undercurrent of heat and sexuality that dive deep into me.

"I'm Elliot," the woman says, holding out her hand.

"Sadie."

"Shall we?" says Kingston after he removes and hangs up my coat.

"Let's." Ryder grins at his brother. "It's been boring so far. Maybe this will spice it up."

I meet his family and his mother is also there. I exchange pleasantries with them all and the conversation is polite and nothing is given away from his mother—not that I expected it.

"Well?" Kingston appears, his mouth at my ear, hand light on my waist. Heat spreads through me from his touch and his scent. I want to lean back into him because having sex with him was a mistake.

The moment I let my guard down, all I want to do is give over to the lust that unfurls in my veins.

"Well what?"

"Learn anything? Because I haven't."

"Your mother is good." I'm fighting the urge to lean against him, aware his brothers watch, all with small smiles. I like his family from our short and polite conversations, and their partners.

None of them fit the mold of the other rich I've rubbed shoulders with. The other rich here who are oblivious to the undercurrents in the room.

His lips brush my earlobe. "Or she's innocent and you're pushing me to think Mother's up to something when she isn't."

Pulling away I turn to face him. This gives me a moment to catch hold of my equilibrium. "But you don't think that, do you?"

"No," he says, glancing past me a moment, "I don't. But that doesn't equate to me trusting you."

"Tell me something I don't know." I take in a breath. "I'm getting some wine."

With that flimsy excuse, I pull free and get one, shifting back as much as I can into the shadows, and then I get directions to the bathroom.

I'm not about to use the one on this floor. I don't even want the bathroom. I'm here on a little mission.

Scarlett and Zoey are wearing their jewels and I can't examine them without things getting awkward. But Elliot isn't wearing hers, so I want to find their bedroom.

Athena said something to me about the photos and the way they're made. The touch is lighter, more delicate than other Mininchi pieces.

I've seen some of those, up close and in person. Held them, studied. I haven't seen a Sinclair Mininchi in person. I want to. I need to.

The bedroom is the fifth room I go into on the third floor. I know instantly it's their private floor, and this is their bedroom. It's a mix of art deco and modern. All class, and with beautiful plants, too. But I want her jewels. Not them specifically, just one.

There's a chance, of course, they keep them in a safe, but I don't think so. This family isn't over the top even though they drip more money than normal people can dream about.

Elliot would wear jewels, but they would always be a deliberate thought and I'm thinking the engagement is new, so that's her jewelry of the evening. And her dress is simple, elegant and with the kind of lines that don't demand adornment.

I rarely wear jewelry, but that's me. Maybe she's similar, I don't know her. But I like getting in the heads of the people whose homes I'm in. Whether it's for robbing or protecting, it's all a puzzle that begs to be solved.

Elliot isn't used to being center of attention, but she's not precious. Her jewels will be away, but I'm betting her necklace—the Sinclair piece—won't be. It'll be something to see, to admire, to touch because it was given to her by Ryder. She'll wear it, but on special occasions and this isn't special to her.

On an old art deco desk is a mirror, old and exquisite, and in front of it is an ornate box and a beautiful carved blackwood dish.

In that is the necklace.

I smile as I pick it up and turn it over in my hands.

There's no doubt in my mind this is a Mininchi. Or meant to be.

It glows with a delicate touch, and its beauty can't be captured in full from photos.

But Yia-yia is right.

Still, I'd love to have these. I covet them in a way I've never coveted jewels before. I'd keep them, and it would be so easy to slide this into the hidden pocket of my full skirt.

The air shifts around me and my heart starts to beat fast as I close my hand around the necklace.

I look in the mirror.

And meet Kingston's gaze.

He isn't smiling.

"What the fuck are you doing, Sadie?"

# Chapter Twenty-Three

## KINGSTON

Sadie's gaze holds mine.

She doesn't panic, doesn't tumble out excuses at me. Doesn't look startled.

And I give her points for that, I really do, but anger builds in me as she turns, still holding the necklace.

"I wanted a closer look."

"With your hand? Maybe by hiding it somewhere?"

She looks stunning, elegant, romantic. The black satin dress has a full skirt that ends above her ankles, and she wears stacked heels. The top of the dress is fitted with a plunging V-neck that is lovely rather than obscene. It hints and doesn't overtly display. The spaghetti straps cross in the back into a pattern that makes up the top part of her bodice.

But stunning isn't the same and trustworthy and whatever tenuous ways I was making there, teeter.

"No," Sadie says. She opens her palm. "I wanted to touch it, feel it, study it. And it's not really something I can go and ask."

"Of course you can. We can. Or could have."

She nods but makes no move to put the piece back. "You want your mother to know I want to look at them?"

"Honestly? I really don't care."

"Don't you?"

I cross the bedroom, stopping halfway across the room because I'm interested to see what her aim is. I'm aware her turning up at my place and getting me here was definitely an excuse for this.

The eye fucking she gave when I opened the door? That barreled into her. Me, too. Because it took all I had not to throw her to the wall, drop my shorts, push up between her thighs, and wrap those long legs about me and plunge to the hilt into her.

The sheer effort it took for me not to get a raging hard on?

Steel will and stubbornness on my part.

Both things I clung to with the thinnest of string.

And now?

There's a reason I'm standing this far from her.

But still...

She looks so goddamn good.

The pulse in her throat throbs. Her eyes are dark, a spark of sheer defiance and lust in their centers and I'm beginning to think I have no problems with fucking her here and now in my brother's room like some randy fool.

But I'm not going to do that. That's why I'm standing this far from her. Though I'm suspecting it isn't far enough. I don't know what would be.

"Okay," I say. "You got me. I do care. As in, I care if she's dabbling in some kind of bullshit to fuck me over. Which I think we can agree, she isn't."

"I don't know your mom."

"Don't you?"

She smiles and it's a little feral. My blood pressure ticks up. "I work for you."

I let it go because any transaction between them isn't about fucking me over. It might be my mother playing games, but she's not out to get me.

"So you do."

"Aren't you going to ask me," she says, opening her palm and holding out the necklace, "if I came to steal this?"

"I think I did."

"Your conclusion?"

"I think you're good enough to do it, but you're also not that stupid."

For a moment, we both look at it, and the stones glint in the light. For a moment, I think she just might slide it in a pocket or down her top or something, just to fuck with me.

But she doesn't. Sadie turns and slips it back in place. "I wanted to look at it to get a feel. I need to be able to tell—"

"Athena?"

She casts a narrow-eyed glance at me. "Yes."

The look is dangerous and sexy as all get out. "How is that coming along?"

"It's coming."

I gesture to the door and she starts to stalk past me, but I catch her arm and pull her in close. "Don't test me by stealing from my family."

Her lips press together and the withering look she sends me tells me she can do just that and she also won't. And that it pisses her the fuck off that I said that. "I'll do what I want."

"Yeah," I say, breathing in her sweet and smoke laced scent, "you will."

And we go back down to the rest of the soiree.

I forget what the charity is. This is probably some offshoot for my slightly reformed, black-hearted brother, Magnus. Who is so far from the ruthless and driven man I know, that sometimes I have to take a step back. It's not immediately obvious if you don't know him, and it's way more pronounced when he's with Zoey, the woman who stole his heart.

He's still hard as nails, still driven and ruthless but with rounder edges. And the things he does for the community in Brooklyn where he's building his vision of the future of tower complex living is real. Because of her.

Even work focused Hudson has loosened up with the bubbly, talkative Scarlett. He's wound in knots and relaxed. The former is her pregnancy, the latter all her. And of course there's my lothario brother who fell hard. Ryder still charms women, still flirts, but his eyes, his soul, they're for Elliot. And it's not just a new love thing, much as I loathe saying it. It's one of those long-term things.

For the lot of them.

Idiots. That's what they are.

My mother chooses that moment to come up to me. "Don't be a sour-puss."

"Go away," I say.

She laughs. "It's the look on your face when you observe your brothers. You could have your own happiness."

"I'm happy. I don't need some woman there, so keep out of it."

"Do you see a woman with me wearing some kind of bow?"

I give her a long, hard look. "To be brutally honest, I wouldn't put it past you."

"Kingston, dear, I wouldn't subject some poor creature to you. But just so you know, not all women are the one who hurt you all those years ago when you were not more than a boy."

Turning, I stare at her. "He told you?"

"Of course your father did. We didn't have secrets, not after I left him."

"You left him?"

"Your father was a man who didn't get his priorities straight. Not for a long time. Don't let pride get in your way."

Ahead of me, through some people, Sadie's in conversation with Ryder. I don't bother with whatever life lesson my mother's attempting to impart, I excuse myself and make my way over to Sadie, who's in the middle of asking my brother all about his security.

Whether she's doing this to fuck with me, or sell him services or whatever, I don't care. I want to put an end to it. "If you'll excuse us, it's time to leave."

We make our goodbyes and I call a car and bundle Sadie into her coat. Let them think whatever they're thinking. I just don't want to be there anymore. It's not until the car pulls up at her apartment building that I turn to her and break the silence.

"Don't pull shit like that, Sadie."

"Like what?"

I breathe out and keep my hands to myself through sheer effort. "Like you were probing my brother for information. Like you were casing the joint."

"Come on." She folds her arms and glares. "I wasn't doing that. I don't do that."

"Anymore?"

She eyes me like she wants to smear my insides on the road with her bare hands. And I probably deserve that look. Still, doesn't make her innocent. At all.

"I was talking to your brother. He asked, that's all. Believe me or don't believe me, I really don't care. Now, I'm getting out of the car and you're staying there."

Fine by me. I let her go. "Sadie?"

She stops as she's about to close the door. And she waits.

"We'll talk tomorrow."

"I can't wait."

As I head home, I think about it all. We're no closer to finding the tiara or who has it. On the surface, I do believe her, after all, Ryder's a phone call away. But she didn't spend time talking to my mother and finding her with the necklace sits uneasy for all that her excuses made sense and still do.

Thing is, they're excuses.

Whether they're also the truth...time it seems, will be the thing that shows me the path.

My brother does call me the next day, saying he wants her information. Said Sadie would put him in touch with someone for his buildings. I'm betting her ex. It leaves a sour taste when it shouldn't even touch me at all.

Mother? She's evasive. I call and when she manages to call back two days later—like she leads the kind of life I do where sabbatical means a shit ton of work which I'm plowing through—she needs to, apparently, keep it brief.

I let her. What am I going to do? Hold the woman captive? She'll talk when she wants and right now, she doesn't. Apart from reminding me what rides on all this.

Sadie I talk to, too. There's nothing on the horizon there, but she tells me to keep faith. Those are words she actually uses, like we're nothing at all and she's giving me her little professional pep talk and it pisses me off.

Actually, I'm so annoyed I leave the deal I'm working on in the hands of one of my most trusted. It takes a brief email to set the ball rolling there, and then I'm up out of my home office and heading across town to see Sadie.

It's a warmer day, no sign at all of that light snow we got, and the sky is bright and blue with fluffy clouds that don't fit in with my mood at all.

If it did, I'm sure it would be a wild and dark storm.

This time, I ring her doorbell and wait for her to let me in, while two tattooed and pierced people sitting on the stoop watch with interest. I ignore them.

"Yes?"

"Buzz me in if you know what's good for you."

She doesn't say anything for a moment and then she sighs and the door buzzes open and I'm at her front door in record time.

It's open and she's leaning against the doorjamb in black jeans and boots and an old, fitted The Birthday Party T-shirt that's fraying at the edges and slightly gray from way too many years of washes.

"I was going to call you," she says, moving away and leaving me to follow.

I do just that and slam the door shut behind me, my anger around me like a cloak.

"Yet you didn't."

"Why are you so pissy, Kingston? I'm not saying you can't rock the vibe, but I don't get why."

"You."

She turns, holding a folder in her hands. Her gaze is hot on me as she looks at me. "This might lighten your mood."

I take the folder. I want to tell her it's her in so many ways. I want to put my hands on her. I want her mouth. Her pussy. I want...fuck, that's why I'm so pissy as she puts it. I want her and she's been acting like nothing ever happened between us. Like she doesn't want me, too.

I've wanted women who haven't wanted me. I've wanted round two when they only ever wanted round one. It's happened. Not often, but it's happened. And if that were the truth here, I'd live with it. Move on emotionally—not that my emotions beyond want and lust and need are involved—and be fine.

But that's not the case.

The air between us sings and crackles. It hums. And she looks at me with hunger. She can't hide that anymore than I can.

That's why I'm so fucking pissy. She pretends in the worst way possible and then fucks me with her eyes. And yeah, I want all the rounds with her. I want her moaning and shaking apart. I want to pound her. I want to kiss her everywhere. I want to worship and possess. I want her in every way possible.

And I think she wants the same from me.

"Kingston," she whispers. "Don't."

"Don't what?"

"Look at me like that. You know we're a bad idea."

"We're the absolute worst," I say and go to her.

I don't touch her, just open the folder.

We look at each other and she hands me something else, wrapped in cloth. I take it, too, and open it.

And suddenly the lust morphs into excitement of a different breed. "Is...is this the fake?"

"Yes. It was delivered this afternoon, before you arrived."

"Oh holy fuck."

"Pretty much what I said. Those are the photos of it to show."

One of the photos is with the date, and also with today's paper.

I set them down, still holding the fake. "I haven't ever seen the original except in photos, but this looks good."

"Better than good." And Sadie starts pointing out things. "There are little scratches on the original in the photo. And there's the engraved stamp always left on his work. As a piece, this could fetch a handsome price. It might be better than the original, but since we haven't seen it, we don't know. It should do."

She's right, it should. I let her take the tiara and she wraps it and sets it back on her desk and picks up another envelope.

"What's that?"

"For Jenson, like we planned. Can you get a courier?"

I whip out my phone. "I'll have one of my subsidiaries here within the half hour." I rub a hand down my face. "Looks like we're going to be spending some time together."

And I sit down on her sofa, getting to work on making sure this goes well.

It takes less than an hour for Jenson to call me. I glance at Sadie, who rises from her desk and comes to sit next to me. We've been quiet, both working, keeping our distance, but as I set the phone to speaker, that's gone.

"Kingston, I got the photos you sent."

"I have it."

There's a silence, long, loaded, and finally Jenson says, his voice low, "So I see. Uh, just, just be careful."

"What are you saying? You said I had to have it found and I hired someone. We found it, so…"

"Kingston, listen, there might be a fake. We'll need to make sure."

"You think I have the fake?"

"I don't know. I'll call you back in the next few days, as it's not due here yet until your birthday. Just be careful."

He hangs up after droning on about legalese and what we'll have to do when that time comes. He wants it on my birthday and not before. Sadie's gaze meets mine.

"That was weird," she says. "A stipulation? The waiting?"

"Who the fuck knows."

She smooths her hands down her thighs. "It buys us time."

"Does it? Because from where I'm sitting, it feels like Jenson is up to something." I take a breath. "Maybe it's him and not my mother behind this."

"You think your father's attorney stole the tiara?"

"I know my mother wouldn't." It just doesn't fit. And I try and work out what she's saying. "So it has to be him, right?"

But Sadie shakes her head. "I don't think it's Jenson."

"How would you know?"

"Because," she says softly, "I'm not sure it's missing."

# Chapter Twenty-Four

## SADIE

The expression on his face is one of disbelief, and I don't blame him.

"What the fuck are you saying?"

"What I said." I lean forward. "I mean, I don't think it was stolen."

"Then someone's doing this deliberately. Playing games." His hands clench like he wants to destroy something, and his jaw is set with steel. "I don't care if it's some game with me, but the company on the line? That's taking it too far."

I lick my lips, trying to sort my thoughts. And I place my hand on his arm. "I didn't say this was the kind of game designed to destroy you. And I don't even know what game it is, or whether—"

"It was something planned."

He doesn't say this to finish my thought as I was about to say 'or whether I'm right in this', but since Kingston's drawing conclusions from the dangling strands, I follow them.

His father, he's thinking his father might have set this out.

"At this point," I say, "it doesn't matter if there's a game or not. We pushed and we got a result. Right now, getting this to them matters. On your birthday."

"Fuck all that. I'm not playing." He stands, moving away from me.

"I'm not sure that's an option, Kingston."

He glares, but the rage isn't for me. It's the kind with no target, not one he can reach and the frustration is palpable. Inexplicably, I want to soothe him. I don't move from the sofa.

"Whether it's a test or not, whoever is behind this, right now it doesn't matter. And I don't think you not playing is an option," I say again. "Not if you want to make sure the family flagship company stays in your family's hands. And not if you want the actual tiara."

"Unless, of course, it is stolen."

"Then we'll get it back. In the meantime..." I spread my hand to take in the fake. "We have that."

But Kingston isn't really caring about that. And I should have known. He's a man who won't rest until he has answers. Until he's satisfied. I shiver. It's a shiver made of begrudging respect and not a little lust. A man like him, oh yeah, does turn me on.

I drag my head and libido away from that and focus on the issue at hand.

"Jenson said fake. He knows." Kingston swipes a hand through his dark hair.

"There are two options here. Jenson knows because he has the tiara, or he knows there's a fake out there—"

"Which is suspicious."

"I never said it wasn't. I'm looking only at what we have."

"You said two options," he says. "What's two?"

"That he's bluffing." I shrug. "We won't know until we do, but this could explain why we've heard about it but not seen it. Why it hasn't shown up for sale or why someone hasn't bragged they have it."

"Of course they fucking brag."

I look at him. "You know this from your vast experience?"

"I know a lot of rich people." Kingston says this in the way others talk about crossing the road. "Collectors brag."

He has a point, but these collectors...they don't brag to all and sundry. It's a small set, and I tell him so.

Kingston leans against the wall, his expression hard, bordering on brooding, but I know he's sorting things in his head. I might not know the man, but I know him, at least, part of him. How his fascinating brain works and I wait.

"Thing is," he says, finally, "if it's not missing as in stolen, then Jenson—" he straightens "—or my mother, knows where it is. Otherwise, why the actual fuck are we waiting for word on some sale?"

"I said 'think'. It's the operative word."

"We go ask them."

"Cool, no really. You've got it all worked out."

"Hey." A small smile appears, even though his eyes remain dark and cold. "I'm the one with everything on the line. The one who should be getting frustrated, not you."

At least he's not flinging accusations at me like bullets. The type saying I'm behind it. Which I'm not. This shit wasn't in the brief job description from Mama Sinclair.

I shift my head back into the game. "We both know that avenue will be met with a big fat nothing, otherwise we'd have it and we'd have parted ways. Something I'm behind, just like you."

The smile still doesn't go anywhere near his eyes.

"And I could be wrong with me thinking these things, Kingston." I get up and start pacing to think. There's something off, and we both know it. The same thing that's been off for a while and now it's starting to smell. "You've spoken to Jenson before, and he's what? Been sounding like that?"

"No."

"So far, both he and your mother have been cucumber cool."

"My mother has." The smile's vanished now and he comes to stand in front of me, effectively stopping my pacing. "Jenson's been Jenson. This is the first real time I've heard him flustered in this way, like he's a step away from Jenson's version of panic. If I'm saying I have it, then he's involved."

I nod, letting his words slide through me, trying to ignore the heat of him, the fact he's so close and if I reached out, I'd touch him and then... "If he stole it, which is what you're implying."

"That's what I'm saying, Sadie. No implied."

Slowly, I let out a hiss of air. "If he did take it, then why not let you pretend you found it, or think you had?"

"You're the one who came up with the theory it's not stolen or missing." He rocks on his feet a little. "What if he thought I was getting it evaluated?"

All my feelers I have out lead places that end up at dead ends. Which never happens to me. There's something so off, and maybe I'm too close. I don't know. "So, we say it has been. But not yet."

"Sadie—"

"If he did, then that's gonna light a fire. But first, I think we should also operate that it's missing or in someone else's hands."

"What? They gave it away?"

"I don't know. The more I think about this, the more what-ifs I have. What if they don't know it's gone? What if Jenson was in major financial strife and sneakily giving it away or selling it is the way out, but he doesn't want two to turn up?" I shake my head. "Those are just a couple."

"You've a point, Sadie," he says in that quiet way I've come to realize holds so much, "Occam's razor it, then. Simple. We explore the most likely and we treat it like it is actually going to be sold. So, with the latter we jump on that and then go from there. With the former, he took it or has it and is in financial trouble. I'll get to the bottom of that. Money talks here."

I don't think it's that, but right now all we have is a fake. "Okay, you do that, and I'll explore other avenues. I keep meeting dead ends, but maybe I'm not looking in the right places or asking the right people."

"And here I thought you knew all the scum of New York."

I gaze at him, trying to ignore the sparks that sing inside from him. "Asshole."

"Stop trying to turn me on, Sadie."

"You wish."

"Crazily, I very much do."

Sucking in a deep breath, I say, "I still think something big is going to happen in regards to some kind of underground sale. I just don't know where or what or with who."

"If it's not the tiara, how is that going to help?"

"I don't know. Yet. But we now have options. We have the fake. And we know something has Jenson rattled. The fake is what it's meant to be; both a fire under asses and your insurance if we don't get it."

I spin away from him and grab my coat and throw his at him.

He asks, "How? And where are we going?"

"How? Even if they have the real one, I say they because I'm bundling your mom in this, but if they have it, then it will appear that day, so you'll fulfill your part of the quest."

"I still want the damn real one."

"I know."

"So, where are we going?"

I pick up my bag and open the door as he pulls on his coat. "You're doing whatever you're doing, and I'm doing my thing. Alone."

"No."

Annoyance ticks through me, but I tamp it down. "I know you don't trust me, but this time, you need to. I'm asking you, too."

After a long moment, he nods. "This one time," he says, and then he's out the door and gone.

I lock up and am on the street and in a cab, heading to midtown when a text comes in from one Ryder Sinclair about security. Or else it's an excuse to get information from me for Kingston.

He wants to meet, his offices, which are midtown. It might not even be his main one. These Sinclair brothers have businesses all over Manhattan. I agree to meet, and after a half-second thought I dismiss the whole information pumping.

That isn't Kingston's style.

If he wants to know, he'll ask.

And I know I must be crazy because the whole in your face business of hard-edged Kingston gets me hot and bothered.

Crazy. Capital C.

Since traffic is utter shit, I send out feelers and then call Yia-yia.

She answers immediately.

"Give me a list of who you think would want the tiara," I say.

"What's wrong?"

"That's what I'm trying to find out."

Ryder Sinclair is just as stylish, beautiful, and charming as he was when I met him. He asks me about security for his various businesses, dangles a carrot of hiring me because he wants information.

I play with the carrot a moment. And then a light switches on, bright. He wants information, all right. But not for Kingston.

In his way, he's prodding me to protect his brother, in case he needs it. "You don't want to hire me."

"Actually," he says, reclining in a chair in his office, "I do. My apartment buildings, businesses, need an overhaul. Something good. Crime, you know."

"Uh huh."

I stare at him, his easy, casually flirty smile doesn't slip, though I get the feeling he can be as ruthless as his brother.

"So, you're Kingston's," he says. "Not really his type, but I can definitely see why he'd want you. Smart, beautiful, and more than a handful."

"Listen up, pretty boy, your charm might work on most females, but not me."

He starts laughing. "You sound like Elliot."

And he sounds like a man completely and utterly in love. It's annoying. "I'm not working for you. And I'm not answering your questions about your brother. I'm helping him with his project. That's all."

"Hey, the job is actually for real."

Yeah, I think it is. The strings here are short and obvious and designed that way. "I know," I say, pulling Damon's card from my bag and handing it to him, "but I do apartments. One on one. You want an actual security business. One that makes them. I use them, and refer business there. Call Damon. He's the best."

We look at each other and he says, "You know, Kingston's a good guy."

"I'll call the papers."

He ignores my sarcasm. "King, he... He doesn't let himself get vulnerable, but I get the feeling neither do you. That said, he's got a lot there beneath what you think you see."

"This isn't a personal visit." I step away, towards the door, then turn back. "And I think your brother can take care of himself. He'd also probably kill you for this."

He only smiles.

"Are we done, Ryder?"

"Let King in if you think he's worthwhile. I only ask you don't play with his emotions."

I rub a hand over my eyes. "As I said, I think your brother can take care of himself."

Why people think they know what's going on when it's just attraction—sizzling hot, but attraction and nothing more—I don't know.

"Yeah," he says, "you'd think so."

"This has been nice. Call Damon if you want the best security."

I leave, trying not to run, and not knowing why, because damn, what Ryder said shouldn't make me want to run.

Just like Kingston shouldn't make my heart beat so hard.

Annoyed with myself, I drop by Damon's offices and barge in. He's half in his coat and heading to the door.

"Some people knock."

"Idiots?"

He laughs. "I was going to see you," he says. "Something's going on. I've got a lot of last-minute jobs. Security is being upped for tomorrow at various places. Particular places. People, it seems, are heading out of town."

My senses start to sing. "Time to get out of dodge?" I ask, keeping my voice light.

"No, you know it's not that. And..." He shrugs. "It's certain people. Ones I know you're interested in. My people have been out since five this morning."

There's only one type who'd be heading out and want a security upgrade.

I wait because I know there's more.

"And this. One of my people got this."

He hands me a photo and a slip of paper.

I suck in my breath.

I need to call Kingston.

Kingston is at my place in record time. I've barely got in the door when he buzzes and for some reason my knees go a little weak at that savage expression on his face.

"What have you got that I needed to be here?"

My heart thuds hard.

"People are heading out of town tonight and tomorrow. For an event."

"Don't play games. What people?"

"Collectors," I say. "The big ones."

I explain to him how Damon's upgrading security.

"Okay." He frowns. "But how does that mean something big?"

"They want their things protected. They're being lured last minute and want to make sure no one takes advantage of them being away. Whatever it is, it's big. It's one of the things we've been waiting for. An auction. Masked. So...do you want to go to attend?"

"Try and stop me."

I put my hand on his arm and electricity sparks up and into me from that touch. "Only thing is, it's not in New York."

"Where?"

"Near Wayne National Forest, Ohio. We'll have to fly."

And Kingston grins. "Good thing I'm a billionaire then."

# Chapter Twenty-Five

## KINGSTON

I t takes me a little more time than I'd like to set things in motion with the jet. It's not often I get nervous, but yeah, this afternoon that's heading fast to early evening I'm just that. Getting nervy.

A sleek black car pulls up at the small airfield in Teterboro, New Jersey, home to most of the private jets. And yes, I keep mine here.

My heart starts to tattoo hard against my ribs, pushing that nervous energy up and into excitement as shapely legs appear in low-slung heels.

Sadie places her hand on the top of the door and emerges. The dying sun is setting its glow on her shining dark hair she's got smoothed down. Another look, another Sadie. She's a chameleon in subtle ways, and I like each woman she puts forth.

Could a man ever get bored with her?

He'd have to be dead, and even then…

She's in red, a far cry from her usual black, and it's a Twenties vibe she has going on.

I run my gaze over her as she strides up, the sway of her hips holding my attention a little longer than I'd like.

"Traffic."

"Welcome," I say, "to the joys of city living."

"We're in Jersey." She frowns, and looks up at the Bombardier 7500. "Fancy."

I gesture to the stairs. "I like quality. And this is good for long haul flights as well as short. I don't really need a collection of these."

"Just watches."

"I like watches, Sadie."

Her gaze hits my wrist. "You're not wearing one today."

"With your habit and whatever the fuck we're going to? I left it at home."

I'm wearing a black suit, like she said. Not a tux, but a suit for events I almost never go to unless made.

She climbs the steps and I admire her ass. It's shapely, compact, and I know exactly how it looks, how it feels under my bare palms, my mouth, against my body as I fuck her from behind. It's perfect.

"Stop fantasizing about me," she says without looking back.

It should annoy me she put that together. But it doesn't. I grin and follow her up. "And give up a delightful hobby? Not on your life."

Sadie taps her fingers against the leather of the sofa in the middle section. We both have drinks—Hibiki whiskey in clear, thick glass tumblers. It's a short trip we're making to the middle of nowhere, Ohio, but...

"Not a fan of flying?"

"It's not high on my list," she says. "Especially small craft."

"This is luxury and it's one of the best in the world."

"And small."

"The biggest of the private jets, Sadie."

"Fuck off."

I swallow my grin. Sadie, the woman who it seems lets nothing get to her except perhaps me, hates flying. It gives her a more human edge, a vulnerability. And I like it. Then again, I seem to like everything about this woman I apparently don't like.

And here I thought I'm not the type to lie to himself.

I do like her.

I'm not sure how. In what way. Lust, absolutely. Her mind, her personality, how she looks? They flow into each other, top down, bottom up, and yeah, that's a huge part of her.

But the rest, what it means?

I have no fucking idea. Because I don't trust her in a lot of ways. Right?

"Whatever you're thinking, stop," she says.

"Me?" I sit back opposite her and cross my legs, the smoothness of the ride a slow flow over me. "If say, the tiara is at this thing, won't it push the price up if I appear?"

"If it is. We're going to find that out. The more pieces of the puzzle we have, the more we can discard the ones we don't need."

"The price?"

"You can afford it."

My gaze moves over her slowly. "I can afford most things. The question is, do I want to spend?"

"You can't afford to leave stones unturned, not if you want the truth and the actual tiara. Because that's what you're in this for. We have the insurance, which will let you save the business."

I nod and sip my drink. "Bidding to get my own property?"

Now she smiles. "I never said you had to do that."

"I'm bait?"

"Exactly."

Whatever I thought the place we'd be going to isn't this. We're in Ohio, outside a small, exclusive town where some of the rich like to play because it's not known. But country club with a hint of masked ball vibe is not the image I had in my head.

We stand out, even in masks.

No one says my name, they don't need to, even if they know I'm there, which given my height some do. It's hard to tell who is who with the masks covering most of the faces except mouths, but I recognize one or two. The rest, I have no idea.

They know Sadie, though, and she's striking in red.

Her mask accentuates her eyes, and the cat-like shape to it isn't lost on me.

I'm bait, she said to me on the drive from the private airfield to here. Bait to let those who know that I want my tiara and I'm willing to buy it. It'll push up the price, but...

Well, the rest of what Sadie said is sublime, ballsy, and bordering on diabolical.

If she finds it, she's going to steal it.

After the sale.

"When does it all start?"

"It has," she says as we move about the room. She points to a waiter. This one is new and carries small shots, and he has his entire face covered in mime paint. "The host's right-hand man."

He comes to us and she takes a drink and a napkin. His gaze skitters over me and then back to Sadie. We're in a big room, classic country club vibe and look with the tables and chairs and sofas. A long, sleek bar in the back and subtle and boring music piped in at just the right background level. But when she meets his gaze, she manages to make the entire room shrink down to us and him and he just nods and leaves.

She's good at controlling situations without a word. And I'm more than impressed. I want to mark her as mine.

She doesn't look at me. She's studying the napkin, which looks like it's a small piece of cloth, not paper, and frowns. Words are printed on it and she crushes it in her hand and says, "Come with me and don't say anything."

I swallow a sigh and make a small gesture and we begin the weirdest tour of a room I've been on. I've made the rounds at parties where I don't want to talk to others and don't, all while seeming like I'm not actually ignoring people, but this takes it to a whole new level.

This is slow and leisurely and her fingers brush mine as we walk. Deliberate touches to slow me down, to move me on, and each and every one of them sends a different cascade of heated awareness through my blood.

People talk to each other and some leave quietly. But all through it, I hear one thing over and over: Lower East Side.

It could be anything, and—

"We're going."

I look at Sadie as we head to the door. "Now?"

"It's not here, but I think I know where it is. There's another sale."

It all clicks. "Let me guess. Lower East Side."

It's raining and cold at three a.m. when we get back to Manhattan. Sadie was on the phone and texting for most of the trip back so I got to observe her and she's easy on the eye. Impressive, too.

The piece of material, the bidding form, is in my pocket and I squeeze it like some sort of talisman as we sit in my car outside a run down looking bar on the Lower East Side.

This isn't hipster or the next best thing. It's the kind of place that a certain type go to because the drinks are cheap and the pour heavy and the place is dark and anonymous. I don't need to go inside to know that. I've been to places like this before, because sometimes a man needs to just have a drink. Or conduct business no one else needs to know about.

So the fact so many sleek cars have pulled up and well-heeled types have gone inside is telling.

I don't know these people.

No one here is wearing masks.

Even the dressed down ones have money. I can always pick out money. It's like an aura.

"I'm not staying behind, Sadie," I say for the ninth time.

She breathes out. "This isn't like Ohio. This is the real deal. The other real deal. These are people you don't mess with."

"The tiara wasn't on auction in Ohio. You think it's going to be here. Which, if it's not stolen, means Jenson's selling it."

"We don't know that. I'm going to find out. I want to see who is buying."

"I didn't hear any conversation about the tiara," I say. "Just this part of town."

Her fingers curl about my arm and it's like she's just reached in me and curled them around something deep in my chest. "I know the code words. This is a different sale. As I told you, the other was both legal and illegal. This is all illegal. As in stolen goods. And you need to stay here."

"No."

"This isn't your world."

I look at her hand and then her. And something in me shifts. I place my hand on hers. "It's not yours, either, Sadie."

"You don't know what you're talking about." She tries to pull her hand free, but I don't let her. Her skin is soft and warm and I might not trust her in some ways, but I do in others. And for everything she might or might not have done, this sordid thing isn't her world.

Not now.

And maybe not ever.

At least not in the way she's thinking.

"Sadie, you aren't part of the dregs."

"But that's exactly what I am." She swallows. "Don't romanticize what I've done and who I am because we fucked."

"I'm not. I see you."

"You see what you want to see."

"Yeah, you."

"I know these people. They might have money, but they're from my world. They created it. I just manipulated it."

Something in me hurts because she's speaking soft and there's a wall and behind that wall is pain and the vulnerability her Athena spoke about. Sadie doesn't like people getting close and she shoves. Hard.

But I'm more stubborn than she's ever even begun to assume. And I know this world suits her because they all keep to themselves. They don't want to get in to her center. They want to use and she takes that and turns it.

And if Sadie Hess wanted to rip these people down to owning only used garbage bags, I've a feeling they all deserve it.

These are the type who build fortunes on misery.

"You're not going in alone."

"Kingston."

I squeeze her fingers. "No. Let's use me. Push up that price. If someone has it, let's find out."

And before she can say a word, I'm out of the car.

We go down through a door at the back of the bar. The stone steps and rough walls leading to the basement level are dank and cold. An earthy, musty scent coils around us as I slip my fingers through hers.

Her gaze touches mine and I give her a cool smile. Voices rise and grow louder as we approach a door with a burly guy.

"Raven," she says.

He gives the smallest nod to the door next to him and we go through, into a different world.

It's not pretty. But it's painted black and has low lights with black sofas like it was some kind of speakeasy club.

No one speaks to us, but eyes are on us, hard and greedy. Those are the ones I peg as connected, as criminals who have made it to the top by all kinds of means and now like to collect things that make them feel more powerful, give spice. At least, that's how Sadie put it and I can see it.

Even with those mega rich, the shadowy kind who probably have shares in half my things, who don't commit nasty crimes, but simply don't care where money comes from, I can see they're the type looking for their next claim, their next thrill, and the room is buzzing with Sinclair.

Finally, a thin man of average height and build, with peppered black hair and a lined, hard face peels away from the rest. "You think you're gonna get it back?"

"Let's say I'm interested."

"And with the Raven herself." He turns. "Sadie. I want the tiara, not the man."

"Marconi," she says, and a bolt of electricity passes through me.

Oh holy fuck. This man is more than connected. He's a head of a crime family. Mafioso. I don't need to know him to know who he is, and Sadie knows him.

"Unless he's got more things I want." Now his gaze moves over her in a way that makes me want to rip his throat out.

But Sadie just smiles. "He might, but he's not into sharing those. And everyone here wants the same thing. The tiara."

We get a tight smile and the man moves on and she looks at me. "Don't talk to people."

"I don't think anyone's going to believe I'm a mute."

"Not with that smart mouth, Kingston."

I drop my head so I can use that mouth against her ear. "Keep flirting like that, Sadie, and I'm going to get all kind of ideas."

"Stop that."

"Make me." I slide the knuckles of my hand down her spine, reveling in the thinness of the material, the way her skin is like soft and warm silk. She shivers and my cock starts to pay a hell of a lot of attention.

Sadie turns and those eyes are on me, melting, liquid heat. And I'm caught in them, in her, and I'm not sure I want to find a way out. "Kingston..."

She touches me, her hand coming up to my chest and we're caught in a cocoon of heat and awareness. But she turns away, like she's ripping herself free with all the strength she possesses. And Sadie takes a step back.

Her phone. It's ringing in her small bag, but she makes no effort to fetch it. Instead, she takes another step away, looking around. She goes suddenly still, gaze like a laser on something I can't see ahead where some big men have come into the room and stand. I go to her and I stop too, my breath and lust vanishing.

There it is. Under glass. The tiara. Other jewels are around it in their own glass prisons. And it's as close as we're going to get to the merchandise.

A woman steps out from the small crowd. She's sleek and pretty and ageless and dressed in black old school Chanel. I know, because I think my mother once owned the same outfit. She has perfect blond hair and I've never seen her in my life. She starts calling out numbers and when Sadie shifts, I'm aware she's placed a bet.

The numbers are low, so I'm assuming it's shorthand or code.

I've been to auctions before. But nothing like this silent one where those here know the moves.

In the middle of it, Sadie grabs me and leads me out, and I let her because I don't really know what the fuck is going on.

I wait until we're in the bar. "Did you just spend my money?"

"No. I bid your money. Thirty million."

"That all?"

She drags me outside and my car is still waiting. I open the door for her and follow her in.

Sadie glows, excitement makes her cheeks pink, and her pulse throbs. This shit turns her on, and—

"I didn't want to buy it, Kingston," she says, sliding close. She lifts her face to mine, lips almost brushing against my mouth, her breath warm, her scent evocative as it winds around me like a lover. "I wanted to know who would."

"And do you?"

She slides her fingers down my cheek, a deliberate tease. "Yes."

"So—"

"This is where I take over, Kingston."

"Sadie—"

"In more ways than one." And then she slips her fingers down and over my chest.

Her mouth meets mine.

# Chapter Twenty–Six

## SADIE

I kiss him. Long and slow, and he's completely and utterly delicious. Yeah, I'm buzzing a little from tonight, from keeping everything in check, from finding out some things, some real leads.

But I'm more than turned on by Kingston and the combination of the thrill of the chase of stolen goods, of beating systems and low-lifes at their own game, and it is too much. And I don't want to hold back anymore. At least I don't in this moment.

I come up, and swing my leg over him and sit in his lap. Kingston pushes one hand in my hair and grips lightly against my scalp, pulling me away.

The hand that comes down on my thigh is hot and large and he says, "Are you using me to get off or is this a way to stop me asking you questions?"

"Maybe both."

His eyes glint as he pushes his hand up my thigh, curling it in beneath my dress to brush at the line of my underwear's lace edge. I suck in a gasp as sparks shoot through me, laced with hot need. I roll into him lightly.

Kingston grins. "Just checking."

And he pulls me down for a hot, opened mouth kiss.

It's wild, carnal. He drops his hand from my hair, skimming my flesh as our mouths and tongues come together, a dark and wild torrent of desire that spurs us on, spurs me, and it's like I can't get enough. He grips my hip, holding me as he kisses a trail from my mouth to my throat, and bites down on a tender spot from the last time we fucked.

Licking my throat, he moves his fingers beneath the edge of my panties and along my slick, wet folds, and pushes two into me. He lifts his head.

"Ride me slowly, Sadie. I want to see you come."

I do, gripping his hair, his shoulder, moving my hips as he slides his thumb against my clit, curling his fingers inside me to him, hitting my G-spot and I gasp.

He smiles and it's the most gloriously wicked thing I've seen.

"Ms. Hess's place," he says loudly. Then he lowers his voice. "Keep going, Sadie."

I'm too far gone to stop, inside the sweet pressure is building, pushing at me and I'm teetering on the edge of release, of orgasmic bliss.

"Asshole," I manage to gasp as he moves my hips, moves me on him, with his other hand.

"Kiss me when you come."

I'm starting to shake and I take his mouth in a shattering kiss as I come. And he holds me as I do so, only pulling his hand free when I start to slump and the car pulls to a stop.

I scramble off him, but he takes my hand and opens his door, getting out with me.

"You're not coming in."

"I am."

He is. We both know it. He steps into me, so we're brushed up against each other right at the side of the road in the rain that started again and he kisses me so softly I want to cry.

"Sadie, he didn't see a thing. I hit the talk button."

"I don't care."

"You do."

"Only because if we're going to ever have an audience, I want to know ahead."

He laughs against my mouth and curls his arm around me, and kisses me again. Then he steps back and releases me, only to throw my coat over my shoulders. His is still on his arm as he takes hold of my lapels, smoothing the wet cashmere. "Good to know you think there'll be that time."

"You really are an ass," I say, pulling free.

He takes my hand and leads me to my building as his car pulls away. The streets are empty and magical with the rivulets of glittering silver and gold from the reflected city lights. It's late and I should tell him I need to sleep and that was enough, but he feels good, smells good and I want more.

We don't talk as I unlock the door to the building. We don't speak as we climb the stairs and open my door.

The moment we step in... We don't talk either. His mouth is hot and hungry on mine. It's full of dark promises and filthy demands. I want to demand back, to promise in the moment of more and more and more. I want it all.

He strips me from my coat and dress and I look at him, fully dressed in his suit.

He takes me in. The bra and wet panties. The heels.

Kingston's gaze is more intimate than most lover's touches I've felt. And I deliberately unhook my bra and let it fall to the ground. Then I slide my panties off.

"Beautiful," he says, "you're a work of art, Sadie."

"So are you. One with too many clothes."

"Are you going to fix that?"

I smile and kiss him and he takes me in his arms and lifts me. I wrap about him as he turns and walks me through my apartment. I direct him to my room and he throws me on the bed.

Kingston reaches for his tie.

"No."

"It works better when I can get inside you."

I lift one leg and place my heel on his chest. "I'm taking them off you. But first come here." I drop my leg and I part my thighs and Kingston doesn't need asking twice. He's there, between them.

We kiss like we're at war. We kiss like drowning creatures. And I'm lost in a sea of need for him. I like the feel of him clothed against my naked skin and I undo his trousers and free him.

He groans as I wrap my hand around his erection and I guide him to me. I need it now.

And so does he because he wraps my thighs about him and thrusts into me. It's not sweet. It's a move laced with savage desire and I bite his chin, his throat, his lips. I want everything as he starts to pound into me, and that's all I can think. I want everything.

We fuck hard and fast. We don't play anymore. We just need to reach that pinnacle. His need is palpable and it tastes so fucking good in my mouth as we kiss.

He comes hard, shuddering, groaning my name and it sets me off. And the release for the second time that evening floods me.

It's like I'm alight with power and he controls the switch.

After minutes pass, Kingston sits up and slowly, slowly pulls out of me. Even in the darkness, the light from the living room and from the street outside my window, I can see he's still thick and hard. Glistening with our mingled juices. And I want him in my mouth.

I want him everywhere.

I want him.

Again and again and again.

Kingston strips the rest of his clothes off. "We're not done, Sadie."

"Good."

He's fucking me slow and it's a revelation. I kiss him, undulating my hips to take him deeper into me and it's like we've got all the time in the world.

"Fuck, Sadie, how does this keep getting better with you?"

I push him so we roll and I'm on top now, and I move in that slow, sweet, deep way we've been doing, but now I'm fucking him and it's just as good and he's so right. "I don't know."

My palms are flat on his hot chest. Everything about him is perfect. From his cock to his chest to his face. That doesn't take into account the way he can kiss, or the way he thinks.

"You drive me crazy," I say.

"That's my line." He flips us again so we're on our sides and he has one of my legs pinned, giving him the control as he slides his hand along my other thigh, then lifting it and he looks down at where we're joined, at my pussy clinging to his cock with each long, slow thrust.

I know he's looking. I am, too.

And it's fucking erotic.

It's hot.

"I could fuck you forever," he says, and kisses me.

I'm lost in him again and he keeps that slow drive into me until he's got me teetering again and then he reaches between us, fingers on my clit and I jump and moan.

"Come, Sadie. Come for me."

I can't help it. I do. The pressure builds, and it's too much and I start to shatter, but he keeps going, right through it. He keeps those long, slow thrusts as I dip back down and he keeps playing my clit. I try to stop him as I'm so sensitive, but he doesn't.

"Kingston—"

"I'm not done. You're not done. I want you to lose control of everything but me. I want you to forget everything but me and you and this."

And he keeps going. He's sweating, his muscles like iron. He's keeping himself under control and I grind down on him as he moves again, so I'm riding him, and he whispers words at me. Taunts, demands, pleas.

And that thing inside that still breathes starts to unfurl and I push harder and harder and I come again. And again, but it's still unfurling and I dig into him, my control nothing as all that exists is this feeling of pleasure that lurks at the edges, something so huge, something that's mine, something new, and I start to come in deep, compelling waves and my entire body is one contraction of blinding pleasure so much I'm shouting, I'm crying, I'm whispering and he's losing it, too. And his voice joins mine and we're both gone.

Completely.

Together.

And when it's over all I can think, as he kisses me in slow, half desperate and bone drugging kisses, is that I want more.

More.

Always more.

With him.

It's almost four in the morning when I dress silently and leave. We're at my place, not his, and ordinarily I wouldn't leave a man there. Especially not Kingston.

But I don't have anything he wants. And I need to do this now.

I stop a few doors from my place and breathe in the biting cold air.

I'd love to say we only had sex once and it was quick and boring, but that's not what happened. I did something weird. Unforgivable. I spent the day and next night with Kingston. Even thinking about it sends shudders of heat and awareness through me.

Kingston.

Something…something changed, like something cracked open inside. And I felt the same weird change in him. We laughed and fought and touched and talked. About everything and nothing and all in between.

Half that time was naked under covers, or fucking. Oh, God, having sex with him is a revelation that seems to have no end. It just gets better.

And we watched terrible TV and kissed and made love—no, not that, but it wasn't straight up fucking. It was that slow lose yourself in the other thing that I haven't done since…I don't know. Maybe Damon. And still, this was different, another whole level I didn't know existed.

If I wasn't planted on the ground, tree-like, I'd almost think it could be love.

But it isn't.

He doesn't believe in love.

And me? I don't either.

Love is for suckers and we can't do that again. I don't have room for feelings, but I also can't regret it.

Not at all.

But I have three places spread over Manhattan to break into tonight. I keep going down the street. I'm hoping I'm right. I know who bought it and she'll have it by now.

If I'm lucky, it'll be at the first place I hit.

I get to work.

It's the third place in the heart of Chelsea, and I'm buzzing with the old thrill. No one is here, which makes getting in so much harder. But I'm there, in the tiny room that takes me almost an hour to get into. I can't leave a trace of me being here, which means I have to take my time, and reconnect every alarm layer I disconnect.

Lucky for me, I know Damon's work.

The fake is good. Great. And it might take them a while to know the difference. Hell, I could just keep the real one and Kingston would never know. The fake would be enough to get him what he wants.

But I'm not going to do that.

Not just because it would prolong us working together.

No, I'm not doing that because I can't. Not to him. Jesus, I'm an idiot.

I don't dally, I slide the real one away, and head out. It's almost dawn when I reach my door.

It's locked, but when I step in, I know instantly Kingston has gone. My phone sits on the table. I pick it up and unlock it. Kingston has sent exactly one message, telling me to call him. And there are a bunch from Yia-yia because I still haven't called her back.

I'm about to hit replay on the messages when the skin of my nape prickles. I'm not alone.

Before I turn, I know why Athena's been calling.

He's there. The man I hate. The man I have the kind of complicated feelings for that a therapist would salivate.

"Hello, Sadie. No hug?"

"Hi, Dad. How was prison?"

# Chapter Twenty-Seven

## KINGSTON

Of course Sadie wasn't there when I woke.

It's her MO.

I think she stole it from me.

Given the chance, I might just sneak out on her.

Because the things that happen between us when we're naked is sex on drugs. Sex like sex has never been. It's naked in a way that goes beyond flesh on flesh.

Yeah, as much as I hate to admit it, I'd do the coward thing and run, too.

Even if I was home.

I take a taxi to that place, home sweet home, except it feels empty when I close the door behind me. Empty and sterile in a way it never has before.

Me, the man who likes his solitude. A man who knows what he likes. And my place is my haven.

Or at least, it was, until a woman with a hardcore pixie cut and a mouth that won't quit in more ways than one—my throbbing and suddenly interested cock can attest to that—came into my life.

Shit. If I was an idiot, I'd think I'm developing feelings for her.

Which I'm definitely not.

She didn't leave a note, but then again, she didn't have to. I'm thinking she went after the tiara. And I'm thinking that was also the reason to put space between us.

Fine by me. I'm glad. I need that space, too.

I go into my room and throw myself on my bed, tucking my hands behind my head, trying to keep those images from the last two nights and day at bay.

"Save them for the spank bank," I say to the room.

I wince. I have a horrible feeling that will be an exclusive Sadie kinda bank.

I try to put my brain onto the matters at hand, but I can't. I don't know where all this has got us. No closer to the truth. Closer to the tiara, perhaps.

And maybe that's all that matters. I get it, she sells it and we part ways.

With that, I get up, grab a change of clothes and head to my bathroom.

What I need is to wash her off me.

If only the fucking en suite came with a Sadie remover instead of steam shower, I'd be golden.

If only.

Ever since I got home in the early hours of the morning I've worked, talked with my brothers—fucking Ryder informing me he spoke to Sadie which is Ryder speak for sticking his nose where it most definitely doesn't belong—texted her, been ignored by my mother and worked out.

I'm coming down the stairs from my workout room when I notice that shift in the air, the latent heat and awareness and then, on the very edges, the softest hint of jasmine and smoke.

It's like a sucker punch. I grip the ends of the towel I've slung about my neck and pause, trying to get myself under control.

How Sadie manages to throw me off center is one of life's great mysteries.

Or maybe it isn't.

Because I know how she affects me.

Question is how the fuck does she keep doing it, over and over again when she should be out of my system?

I wipe the towel over my face and then continue down, take the wide hall and go into the wide-open living room.

Sadie stands there, dressed in form fitting black, and she looks, in a word, spectacular.

In her hand is a glass of something, so I go over and get myself a whiskey. It's after lunching hour and I've been up for hours and it gives me something to do. An excuse. Whatever you'd like to call it. But now I'm close and I can breathe her in and take in the heat of her, even as my body reacts because oh yeah, those memories are fresh.

"I'm going to think this is a habit of yours, breaking in here."

"More entering." She takes a sip from her glass and her hand shakes. Most wouldn't notice that fine, almost imperceptible tremor. But I do. "I didn't break anything. I can if you like. Next time."

I laugh softly and lean against the bar. "Next time is interesting."

"Is it?"

"It tells me you'd like to see more of me."

"You have some ego, Kingston."

"Tell me I'm wrong."

"You're not. But like and will are two different things."

I straighten and put my mouth to her ear. "Pity."

Her sharp intake of breath is shaky and uneven, but it has nothing to do with the hum of agitation that runs through her and made her hand shake. I'm so close I can feel that, too.

But I move away and sit in a chair, gaze on her. She turns to the window and the gray outside. It wants to rain again, but so far, it hasn't.

"Was all that just some kind of elaborate game?" I ask, taking a swallow of the Scotch I'm not sure I want, but I savor the burn, and the heat.

"The auctions?" Sadie shakes her head as a rumble of thunder rolls outside and I'm struck with the inexplicable urge to take her to bed. Again.

"You tell me you know who bought it and fuck me when I ask questions."

She finally turns to me a moment. "Tell me you didn't want that."

"You know I did, but that isn't an answer, because every time I asked you told me to trust you or you changed the subject."

"I know what we did. And sure, I used the moment because I wanted that itch you created scratched."

"Did you?"

"No."

"So." I take another sip. "Answer."

"Getting the tiara back doesn't answer your questions."

I nod. "Yeah, but I'll have it and that's a good step. Are you telling me...what?"

Sadie goes to the window and leans her head against it, and her ghostly reflection closes its eyes. Then she breathes out, and her breath fogs out the glass and the ghost. She turns to me. "Something is wrong."

"Like what?" I look at her.

She breathes in but whatever it is she's going to say shifts. I see that in how she straightens and I remember what Athena said about her all over again.

Yeah, we're both experts at locking private gates.

Unfortunately, this is my life, my money she's using, so I need to know what's there behind her gates.

"Should I remind you that you work for me?" I ask.

Sadie's expression turns cold, but the agitation is still there. "No. You don't need to do that, Kingston."

"So maybe you want to explain yourself, starting with your plan."

She presses her lips together a moment. "Getting or not getting the tiara, you mean?"

"Let's cut the not out of that."

Her eyes narrow and she starts to pace, a surefire sign there are a million things going on in her head. "You'll get what's yours. You always do." She takes a deep swallow of her drink, the shake a little more pronounced, and it sends ice through my veins. "But the rest of it is something we need to understand."

"It's more want, unless you think it's a setup."

"I don't know. That's the problem. I keep pivoting from one thought to another and everything is neat and simple until it isn't and...are we looking at this in the wrong way?"

"What do you mean?"

"The amount paid for the tiara was a hell of a lot. We're talking hundreds of millions."

I shrug, even though nonchalance is as far from me as it's ever been in my life. "Everyone in there can afford it and when I have it back, providing you don't steal it from me, I can double that. After I get it evaluated."

"You're a fucking bastard, Kingston."

She doesn't say how dare you. She doesn't say I wouldn't steal it. No. She throws an insult.

It's in line with how she is, so why the fuck do I get the feeling Sadie's evasion means something?

"So you've told me. Do you have it?"

Sadie stills. "Do I look like I have it on me?"

Again, it's in what she says, down deep. Or what she doesn't say. I get to my feet, intent on getting to the bottom of her little games, finding out why she's agitated enough I can see it. But she jumps in.

"Kingston, did you hear anything back yet about Jenson?"

"Not yet. It takes a few days. I'm not breaking any laws. Innocent until guilty is still a thing, so I'm fast tracking legal avenues. With his layers of lawyerly ways, it's taking a little longer. He clearly knows how to circumvent certain tax laws."

I got that report when I went through private emails on my separate server. And I almost laugh. He's also not breaking laws, bending, but not breaking. I didn't know the old conservative guy had it in him to play that way.

"Okay. So if we're looking at this wrong, let's look at the tiara. I've only seen the necklace and it's beautiful. So why hide things like this away? From what I've read of your father he wasn't flashing your money, but the jewels are heirloom, they're something that should have been on display in some way, not hidden and buried beneath rumor. Did he say why?"

I shrug again and come up to her. "I'll play, Sadie. For now. No, he didn't say. We never knew if they were real or lost to time or just something once worn and labeled Sinclair. They were talked about, whispered about, but he and our grandfather never said a word about them existing outside something that might once have been family bling."

"Don't you think it's strange?" I'm close enough I can see the slight dilation of her pupils, the tiny flutter of her pulse point in her throat, the softening of her mouth as she looks at me. And my guts twist and libido hums.

"I wouldn't know. It just was."

"These are things you yourself told me bring a certain something to the family and Minchini is a name to be revered. So?"

I breathe out and shake my head, and I step away a little. "For some reason we don't know they were hidden, and it seems deliberately so. In the family there were whispers from aunts and cousins of the rumors. Never around my father, but kids hear things. You name it, we heard it. They were cursed, so were locked away."

"Do you think your father would buy into that?"

"Fuck no. He liked money and had no time for pretty stories."

She raises a brow and I scowl.

"Fuck you, too."

"You have."

I half laugh. "The tales ran the gamut from bad luck to loss in a card game, to being stolen long ago. There was one of them being melted down to solidify the family fortune, a rumor which brought the old man out in hives because of how it made his family look. Christ, Sadie, you name it, I heard it. Like they were even fake and made by Reardon, Minchini's one-time apprentice. That was a popular one."

"I've never heard of a Reardon, but if so, then it could make them either worth even more or nothing."

I finish my drink and set the glass on the bar. "If it was true."

"If."

Our gazes crash and I reach out and take her drink, setting that down, too. And I close in again. "Where is the tiara?"

"The jeweler, if it wasn't Minchini, was talented enough to pull off his style and touch."

"Like your Athena."

She smiles softly. "Hers is only made to look old. From the necklace, the workmanship is of the right era and..."

"What?"

Now she shrugs. "Whoever made them might have been Minchini or someone with more talent. Because they're the best of all his jewels."

I trace the shape of her lips. "And here I thought you only saw the one piece."

"I did."

"You said they."

She moves in, brushing against me and places her hands on my bare chest. It's an invitation and a dare. And I'll take both.

"Maybe I stole back your tiara."

"Did you?"

"Or maybe I just saw the photos."

"Or you're lying to me." I slide my thumb in between her lips, into that hot, wet goodness. "I do know two things. You're hiding something."

The guileless expression on her face tells me I'm right. "And the other?"

"I'm going to kiss you."

I move my thumb, running it slow down her chin to circle her throat with my hand, and then I take her mouth in a slow, deep kiss.

The world spins slowly when I lift up. And she's breathing hard and fast. I'm already erect. I throb with wanting her.

"That it?" she asks, as she slides one hand up to my nape and the other down to my cock. "Or is there more?" And she squeezes me, making me groan. "I'd like more."

"Come to bed with me, Sadie."

"Yes."

And I kiss her again, this time a dark, erotic kiss that leaves us both shaking. I take her hand and lead her out of the living room and to my bedroom and strip us both down.

We touch and explore each other, taking our time, an urgency building.

Right before I lose myself in her, I know this isn't over.

I'll get to the bottom of whatever she's hiding.

No matter what.

# Chapter Twenty-Eight

## SADIE

That was stupid. I can't get it out of my head and I can't one hundred percent get behind it because sex with Kingston could become as important as breathing air.

"Hey."

I look at him, halfway to getting dressed. I hold my top. "I know, I know. I get it. That was sex. And I'm with you. I'm getting out of here and back on the case and then I'll be out of your life."

"Sadie?"

"Yes?" I scowl at him.

And he smiles. It's a heartbreaker of a smile. He hooks a finger into my lycra laced top and pulls it away, flinging it down. "I'm not asking you to be out of my life."

"Kingston." I close my eyes. "You don't want me."

"I think we know that's a lie. Open your eyes and come back to bed."

"We have a ticking clock."

"And we have the fake and not much we can do unless you've got a big, bad confession. Do you?"

I do. My father is there, suddenly in my head, or rather, his visit. It would be so easy to tell this man about it, the way I felt like I was ten. The manipulation that crawled over me. Or the fact I didn't listen to Athena telling me his parole was coming up.

I didn't think he'd get out, I could say. Hell, maybe I could tell Kingston my charming father, the man who tried to make and break me down into an image of him, had been nothing but nice, contrite, and vices closed in.

Nice and contrite and it was all a threat without a single word of malice.

I could say that Trevor Masters turned up and I felt like I was a scared child again. One whose eyes had finally been opened.

I could tell him every sordid thing I'd done, the kind of crimes he'd made me complicit in that I worry that stains won't come off my skin. That they'd sunk deep and down into my bones.

Shit, I could even tell him how I got my hands on my birth certificate and when I could, legally changed my last name to my dead mother's name. A woman who'd run away, died in childbirth, or was a drug fiend my father saved me from. Take a pick because Trevor liked to change the story to suit his mood and every single one was true in that moment because he had that gift of turning anything into the truth.

I don't even know what happened to her. And years ago I stopped looking. No death certificate existed but that didn't mean anything, just she didn't die in childbirth. And...forgive me, I've stopped searching, stopped caring. I have myself. And Athena. And I don't need or want anything else.

I could say all this.

I don't.

I don't say a word. I take in that smile, the naked torso, and the offer in his eyes.

If anyone could make me believe in a better world then it would be him.

But I made my own world.

And Kingston doesn't make me any kind of offer except here. And now.

"No confessions," I say. "Not one. Except I don't want to go. Not right now."

"Jesus fucking Christ. Are we on the same page?"

I smile and go to him and he pulls me down over him and kisses me.

I'm ready to take the offer of sex. It's warm and real and there.

But he doesn't move to touch me except hold me against him, and stroke my cheek as he kisses me again.

"What...what are you doing?"

He laughs. "Holding you. Until my mother calls back and until I get word on Jenson, and you go and find the tiara, then I can think of other things to do with our time."

"I'm going to—"

"Stay here. For a bit. Please?"

And, so I do.

We laugh and joke and I let myself take this sliver of happiness. Because that's what it is.

I stretch. "This is nice," I say quietly, much later.

"Yeah, it is." He slides his fingers through my hair. "Sadie, I—"

Kingston's phone rings.

"Hold that thought."

"It's your thought, Mr. Billionaire. I'm not paid to hold your anything."

He just gives me a look that makes me laugh. I don't know why I feel light inside. But then he glances at his phone.

"Shit, I need to deal with this." With a groan, he answers. "Yeah? Okay, okay, give me five."

Kingston gets up and pulls on jeans, puts the call on mute, and comes back and kisses me.

"The fairy tale is ending?" I ask.

He sighs. "For now. I really have to take this or else I'd tell them where to go. We're not finished. Stay here. Please?"

I don't answer, and he leaves, pulling on a sweater as he does so.

When a door closes, one I'm sure is his office, I get out of bed and into my clothes so fast I could win a medal. I race out of the bedroom and down the hall and open his door. I cross the landing to the elevator and keep pressing the call button until it arrives.

Like a small, scared child, I'm running away. It's what I do with him.

The doors close and I let the air out from my lungs. I'm not staying to hear him tell me this is just sex. I have things to do.

And I didn't tell him I have the tiara. My father turned up, and I got scared. I mean, I—

I stop.

I have the tiara and it wasn't my father's unexpected visit stopping me from telling Kingston.

Suddenly my legs give out, and I slide down the wall of his private lift and hit the bottom.

It's not my father. Not at all.

Sure, I went in there, upset about Dad, but...that isn't why. I'm planning on giving it to Kingston. My promise to the low life isn't needed now, and I only wanted to see what information I could get from him.

No.

When it came down to it, I didn't tell Kingston because I don't want this to end. And it's coming to an end. His birthday is coming fast. I could get Athena to make another fake. We could continue the chase for it. Or I could try and drag out the sale.

I don't want this to end because I like him.

Oh. Fuck. I have feelings for him.

I probe them. Carefully, like with a bad tooth. But like a bad tooth, they hurt and feel too big, too there. And I don't know what to do.

For the first time, I don't know what to do.

Yia-yia will tell me to be honest. To let him in. She damn well likes Kingston. She told me he was arrogant and shifty and all the things I am. And then she floored me and said he had a good heart.

I haven't let myself near that.

Not until now.

I glance up. I'm fast approaching the lobby. I grab the rail and pull myself up, legs still shaky.

I didn't lie about trying to get to the bottom of the rest, because I know he wants that. But I'm going to need to get that tiara from where I hid it away. Get it and do the right thing for once, because come what may, I like him.

Maybe more than like him.

And maybe...maybe that isn't a bad thing.

"The one thing you were never good at, Dad," I say as I step into my apartment, closing the door with the scratch marks on the locks, "is B and E."

My father comes out of my bedroom. He's been through my place and he hasn't bothered to hide it.

I'm such a fucking idiot to think I took care of things.

Because he has something in his hands. And it turns my blood to ice.

"I gave you a lot of money," I say in a deliberately unconcerned tone. "Breaking in and trashing my place is a crime. And you're on parole."

He laughs. He's older, gray. Fit from no doubt working out in prison. But he always liked to look good. He probably has a piece who he sucked dry while in there. Men like him always find a way to land on their feet, even behind bars. I really want to hate him. But it's complicated.

One thing I know is I don't like him. At all.

"You wouldn't turn in your dear father, would you, Sadie?" He smiles and lifts the tiara, studying it. "Because I know all your secrets. Ones the police would be interested in."

I don't bother asking how. He doesn't have evidence because I'd have heard from him long before this. "That isn't yours."

"Isn't yours either."

"It could be." He runs his fingers over the intricate stonework. "Fetch a good price."

I want to snatch it from him, but I don't. "It won't. It's fake."

"I don't believe you." He grins then. "I followed you. Sadie, I recorded you. It'll be in the papers soon and I'll be a hero."

"You'll turn your daughter in?" What am I saying? Of course he would. Trevor Masters only loves one thing more than money and the grift. And that's Trevor Masters. "You'd have to turn that in, too. And these rich people aren't really into handing out rewards. Also, it's fake."

"Sadie, this is your father."

"Yes, I know. And I gave you money. If you want more, you'll have to give me time."

He puts the tiara down on my desk, next to my computer, which he's opened. But he hasn't got into it. I can see that. It's locked. Not that he'd find anything.

"Why do I need time? Your boyfriend is a billionaire."

"He's not my boyfriend. He hired me to find the real tiara."

"You're ripping him off?"

"When I get the real one, yes."

The lie comes quick and easy.

But he shakes his head. "You underestimate a parent. You're involved with him and the tiara, if it's real, is worth nothing compared to his fortune."

"Dad, he's not giving you money. He won't. I used him to get information on finding the tiara. The real one. When I do, I'll switch them out and you can have the money."

"You're sleeping with him to get your hands on the real tiara? I taught you better. Milk them."

"Are we done?"

He reaches for the tiara, then looks at me and leaves it. "I'll be back, kid."

The moment he leaves, I start to shake. He didn't believe me. I know that. At least, not completely. But he said something about parents and power and that clicked something into place. I grab the tiara and wrap it, shoving it into my bag. I pull on my coat, sling the bag on my shoulder and head out, hailing a cab.

Faye Sinclair looks up from her computer when her housekeeper shows me into her pretty office. It's feminine and the ornate seventeenth century French desk is real.

If she's surprised to see me, it doesn't show.

"Do you know who my father is?"

She sits back. "No. I—"

"Trevor Masters. And he's just like you've read." I sit without being offered a seat. "He's out of prison. Trying to extort me for money. And he thinks Kingston might care enough to extort even more from him to keep me from prison. For stealing the tiara."

She rests her elbows on the desk.

"But you knew that, didn't you?"

"The tiara part?" Kingston's mother is just as smooth as ever. "It's missing, so..."

I shake my head. "Missing. *Not* stolen. Because it wasn't stolen, was it?" I wave a hand. "No need to answer that. There are some things I don't get. Like why you wanted Kingston to hire me."

"You're the best."

"There are others. And I don't think that's it. But I did work something out from what my deadbeat dad said." I breathe in, then let it out, slow. "I underestimated you."

"People do," she says. "And I wanted Kingston to hire you for his own sake. He needs the right woman."

I stare at her. "I'm not the right anything."

"The reason you know so much about it all, the letters, everything, why your sons have had the added threat of the company over them, is you. They underestimate you and your power. You own most of the shares that keep it in private hands."

"You're good."

"And right." I get up. "Don't play games with Kingston. He loves you, but he won't forgive you. So, here." I pull out the wrapped tiara and an envelope. "The tiara is a little early, but under the circumstances, I don't think it should be in my hands. Or Kingston's."

She glances at them as I place them on the desk. "The envelope?"

"The money you paid me. I don't want it."

"I didn't ask you to betray him."

No, she didn't, she just asked me to slow him down. He'll see it as betrayal. None of that is why I'm giving the tiara to his mother and not to him. And it's really simple.

I don't trust him.

Kingston is ruthless, out for himself and a cynical bastard, and I'll never forgive hm if he hands it to my father in some weird act to keep me safe.

"I know," I say. "But I don't want it in my hands. He asked me to sell it for him. I think it's foolish."

"You can't stop him when he sets his mind to something."

No, but if wants to see me outside this, then I'm not fencing it. I don't want something that can be used as an excuse. I want him to see me for me. And what am I even thinking? That there's a chance? I've lost my mind.

"I need to go."

Suddenly Faye is on her feet. "Take the money."

"I can't. It's...it's not right."

She smiles. But I frown.

"You do know he'll want to have it evaluated," I say. "And you don't want that, do you?"

What if it's actually fake, or not worth what he thinks it is? That's something that'll rip him apart. To be played with. And me... I swallow.

"God," I say, "you made me your accomplice. He won't forgive me if it's not the real deal. He'll think..."

Her smile doesn't fade. "You care."

"No."

"Yes, you do, Sadie. You know what I see? A woman with so much to give and the man you want to give your heart to. You love my son."

Horror sinks down into my marrow. "No. No, I don't."

And I turn and leave, like the hounds of hell are at my heels.

Kingston is waiting at his door twenty minutes later.

"You texted?"

I glare at him. From my father to his mother to this. I'm stretched tight. About to snap. And I don't know why.

I don't want to be here, I do know that. I'm a coward. But the text was a demand. Not an ask. And images of my father bilking him for half his fortune danced through my head. So...

Here I am.

He stares at me, and his expression is odd. I can't read it. Like he's tied himself in extra strong steel doors, shutting everything out.

"You lied."

My skin prickles as I follow him into his mansion in the sky. In his study, he turns to me. Something is up and telling him about the tiara vanishes from my head. "About what?"

"You stole the tiara. I've seen the footage."

I choose my words carefully, because now I get his weirdness. My father visited. "I haven't heard of it being reported as stolen."

"Don't lie to me, Sadie."

"I thought you established I lied already?"

His hand with his phone clenches. "Thing is, you lost out."

"What are you saying?" Panic flutters hard and painful. "I don't have your tiara. Come and see."

"Maybe I will."

We stare at each other and the coldness almost kills me and I know I have to take it and run. "You know, I really thought you'd be different. A pushover when it came to me. The chemistry..." I suck air in deep. "I worked hard at that."

"Did you?"

I nod. "Why go for a tiara when I can go for your fortune? A healthy chunk and I'd be set for life. It would make the trinket look like it came from a gumball machine."

Kingston is silent for a long moment and the pain on his face hurts me. The anger gives me a dark, nihilistic hope. "A grift?"

"Not exactly. More your gold digger move. I find that sort of thing more profitable and law abiding. After all, sex in exchange for money is what all relationships are based on, right? Maybe not money, but it's always an exchange."

"If the gentleman is willing."

"If." I deliberately rake my gaze over him. "And you are."

"Sorry, Sadie, you got it wrong. I don't do exchanges."

"Don't tell me you care."

He smiles tight and icy. "Did you use me?"

My head starts to spin. If I do this, then this is done. Forever. And...

I have to.

"Yes."

The word hangs there in the silence. And it's a death knell. But if it means I make him hate me, then I can save him from my father's sticky, grasping fingers.

So I push further.

"I used you. I wanted your money and a good life and nothing else."

He nods. "I see. It makes sense. You are your father's daughter."

"Maybe I really am."

"And the tiara?"

"I wanted it to start with," I say. "But I don't have it. See, it was a fake. Your tiara is out there somewhere. Or, you might want to talk to your mother. She might have answers."

He nods, a slight frown on that gorgeous face. "And if I don't believe you?"

"I'm telling you the truth, I used you—"

"Fuck you, Sadie. I really don't give a shit about you anymore. I'm talking what matters. My inheritance. If I go to the cops and say you have it?"

I shrug. "Go do that. Search my place, it isn't there, because I don't have it. I sold the fake I made, and gave that money to my father for his part in this. I used you. And now that's done, and you know, I don't want to see you anymore."

Silence slams down on us and I'm drowning because as I say these terrible, horrible words the truth hits me hard.

"I think," he says softly, "you should go. I'm not going to pay you, either."

"Goodbye, Kingston. Sorry about the loss of the company. But that's really on your mother, isn't it?"

I don't wait for him to answer, I just walk out. Like it's broken glass and I'm barefooted. Very carefully.

And inside things crack.

My throat burns hot and my eyes itch and it's not until I'm in the cab home that I give in.

Not to tears. I'm not letting them out.

But I give in to what I've done.

I lied to his mother. To him. To myself.

I did the most stupid thing in the world I've done.

I fell in love with Kingston Sinclair.

And, to protect him, I smashed my own heart, along with any chance with him, to pieces.

We're done.

# Chapter Twenty-Nine

## KINGSTON

**H**er dad comes out from the shadows across the hall.

I don't turn because her words still burn inside me. What she said, how she said it all, put my long ago past into perspective. Back then, I was a kid playing at love and got burned. My ego and pride got crisped up and blacked.

But now?

Oh, fuck me, she's ripped me open and left me bleeding and I...I don't know what to do.

Except deal with this nasty piece of filth who happens to be her father.

I take a breath and rub my eyes, forcing myself back under lock and key. And I turn. The man leans against the door, his lined face wearing a casual smile, a knowing one, like he has me where he wants me.

I didn't lie about the evidence of her leaving that apartment building. Sadie has been busy and not telling me a damn fucking thing, just like I thought.

But—and I need to be real here—as evidence it's non-existent. And no one that bought stolen goods will report that to the cops. He thinks he has me and he doesn't. "You get what you're trying to do, don't you, Trevor?"

"And what's that? Bring you justice?" He straightens.

"We're talking about your daughter you want to throw under a bus. And she says she doesn't have it."

"I showed you evidence," he says.

"Dude, you showed me her leaving a place. That's all. Not stealing."

"She has the tiara."

And even though I'm furious with her for her lies and running out on me when I had to deal with shit, I look at him. "She doesn't. I know this because I have it."

He looks at me like he doesn't believe me. Which is fair, because I'm obviously lying.

"Are you in love with her or something?" Trevor's eyes narrow.

"Or something," I mutter. And then I say so he can hear, "I don't give a shit about her. I do, however, give a shit about a pissant criminal trying to extort money. You asked for a cool thirty million to keep your daughter safe."

"Or hand her over to the police." He eyes me like he doesn't believe me.

I nod. "I could go to the cops with this."

"With what? The fact I came to you about a crime? So, hand over the money."

I merely look at him. "So, you're fine doing this to your kid?"

"I told you. She never visited, so what's she to me? You, I like. I'm helping, but I don't help for nothing."

"No, you don't." I get my checkbook, something I haven't used in a long ass time. I look at him again. "This is the one and only time you extort money from me."

"To keep my daughter from jail."

"I thought you said she's nothing to you." I hold my pen, just above the blank check. "Make up your mind."

"Thing is, this keeps me happy, and her from prison."

"I don't give a shit about her." I go to close the book.

"Pay me, and I go away."

"That sounds like a deal," I say. "Spell your name. I'd like to get it right."

And the idiot does so. Even says it. All for my recording I'm making on my phone. I tear the check from the book and hand it to him. He studies it, more alive than I've seen him.

My stomach turns. The man sickens me and I want this done. "Don't come here again. I just want to get rid of your fucking no good family from my life."

"You—"

"Go or I'll cancel your sweet ass check."

He snaps his mouth shut and pockets the check.

I walk the man out, staying a little too close the entire time. I don't trust him not to take something, and yeah, I'm not above a little intimidation. It's that or beat the shit out of him and I've been told actual violence is not the way.

Besides, my plan is better than instant gratification.

And Sadie...

My chest lurches, aching. Damn her. Damn her to hell and back. She doesn't trust me enough to tell me the truth, she runs. She lies. I fucking hate lies. She tests my patience, and she drives me insane.

And maybe, just maybe, she really doesn't care. Maybe this is just sex on her part, like it was on mine. Was, right up until it wasn't.

I don't know when that started to change. All I know is it's been creeping up on me. Feelings. That's what. Fucking feelings have crept up and they're all shaped like Sadie.

The elevator dings in my private foyer outside and I move through the apartment and sit in my living room, and call the cops.

It takes a bit, but names and influence talks. I call my lawyer, too. They'll all be here soon enough. Sadie's father is going to be back in prison, and fast. I really don't take kindly to blackmail. Or extortion. Or any of the things he tried.

And Sadie? I'm fucking furious with her and her betrayal, but yeah, I'm doing this to protect her, too.

Her father will come for her. Try and get what he can and I don't want that. She probably won't appreciate my interference, but that's just too fucking bad.

I close my eyes and lean back against the sofa. What she said plays over in my head. The whole thing about my mother... I keep thinking about it. And suddenly I know I can't leave it alone. Sadie said a lot of shit that I think might be right. So I make another call.

She answers after the second ring.

"Mother," I say. "I think you and I need a long talk."

My mother looks at me where I'm sitting, making inroads into my Laphroaig. The police and my lawyer have been and gone and finally the woman who birthed me has decided to make a showing. I take another swallow.

"A little early for that."

"Save your bullshit, mother. I'm not in the fucking mood. I'm pretty fucking sure you have the tiara. Or are you changing up the rules? Again?"

She purses her lips. "What did you do, Kingston?"

Interesting. She doesn't ask what do I mean, or what did Sadie say. Just that. And I'm getting more and more pissed off by the second.

"I got her father arrested."

She inhales sharply. "I wasn't... Do you think that's wise?"

"Because you fear for me? Yourself? Or are you worried all your Sadie plans will go south with this reveal?"

She taps her fingers against one elegant hip. "I don't know what you mean."

"Don't give me that crap. Are you trying to set me up with Sadie?"

"She's perfect, Kingston."

"Not your business."

She glares at me. "My children's happiness is my business. And you're talking about having her father locked away. So, I ask again, is it wise?"

"Did you miss the memo? I'm a grown ass man. And yes, it's wise. He'd fuck her over and whoever else he could get his hands on."

"Kingston."

"Don't." I'm on my feet fast and I point at her with my glass. "Her father is a lowlife."

"And Sadie's father. So you want her."

"Don't twist my words. I did this for pragmatic reasons."

She looks heavenward. "This should be good."

"Mother." I glare. "Sadie's smart and tough, but she's also vulnerable and he's her father. So I did it so she didn't have to." I pause and take her in. "Why are you smiling?"

"Because you and Sadie—"

"There's no us. We're not a thing and we won't be."

My mother's smile disappears. "Don't lie to me, I'm your mother. You have feelings. I can see that."

"Says the lying, manipulative woman." Of course I have feelings. I'm human. I don't say this, though. She's going to take that and run with it if I do, and I'm already at the end of my rope. "I don't like you doing that to me. And I don't like her lying for you. She gave you away in the end."

She frowns. "What are you on about?"

"You own the fucking company. You're behind this. And Sadie…" I shake my head, giving over to fury because it's safer than that thing inside me that threatens to shatter. And what I put together from Sadie's words is all true. It's there on my mother's face. So I push some more. I want fucking answers. "She lied. To me. Used me. I know she worked for you."

"Kingston, with an attitude like that…"

"What? There is no me and Sadie, except in your head. And she said the same, didn't she?"

I don't know what I want, but the affirmative answer somehow isn't it.

My mother, however, isn't one to give up easily. "She gave me back the money."

"So?" I smile tightly. "She took the tiara."

"You idiot. She gave it to me. I suspect to stop that man getting it, because I think she was trying to protect you from him. You two are so alike." She picks her leather Chanel bag up from the seat next to her and opens it. Then she hands the tiara to me. "Sit down, Kingston."

"No, I think I'll stand."

"Sit."

I mutter nasty things but sit.

"I made it look like it was stolen. Because I wanted you to learn your lesson."

"And what is that?" I know I sound like a bored prick, but inside it hurts because Sadie is gone.

It's the right thing, but right doesn't stop pain.

"I want you to learn true worth, and making you jump through similar hoops to your brothers wouldn't have cut it. You're not sentimental like them."

I snort. "Magnus?"

"He can be ruthless and cold in a different way to you, but, yes, you were the hardest one to crack." She crosses her arms and taps one sleek shoe, like she's the one who's annoyed here, not me. "And you don't know everything, you fool. I do have the balancing shares. I run Sinclairs, too. And it is all of yours, but you all need to be worthy to have it, otherwise what's the point of it? You don't believe in the heritage."

"Lies."

She sighs softly. "Only for what it can get you. And that's wrong. It's too like your father was. And I don't want that for you. Don't be like him."

"You're mad at him still?"

She looks away a moment. "You have a lot to learn about love."

It hits me then. "You loved him."

Faye laughs. "I never stopped loving him, and even now, I still do. I just got sick of him putting work first, putting the money ahead, the pursuit of power. I left him."

"No, he had an affair."

"That isn't what happened. Not while we were married. He moved on, I didn't. But each break up I was there because your father is and was my one true love. I just couldn't live with the man anymore. Not until he changed. And he did, but it came too late. We were secretly back together when he got the news of his illness."

A terrible sadness comes over her. "When he died, I decided to carry through with his plan...our plan. You see, your father finally saw you were all making your lives like his. And he finally got it, that happiness came from balance. Love and work. Big and little. I didn't want you to keep making those mistakes. Any of you. I wanted you each to find love, and you, Kingston, you were the hardest. It would take someone not just special but someone who could stand up to you and make you laugh and anger you and hold her own. I found Sadie. But before I could do anything, so did you. She's perfect."

"Well, that's neither here nor there, Mother," I snap. "It didn't work. Sadie and I aren't made for each other."

"She said she doesn't love you."

"Good." The pain is almost unbearable when she says that, and she's smiling. I think my mother might be some monster. "I don't love her."

"See? Utterly perfect."

"I'm not discussing my private life with you. Go get your own if you want one. Or I hear those telenovelas offer you all the thrills and passion you could desire from the sidelines. Just keep out of my life. You've got the tiara, and now you've gone and done the pointless thing of handing it to me. You failed. I have this final jewel and the company is safe. So, if you don't mind, I've got an actual empire to run." I stalk up to my mother. "And I'm going to get this thing evaluated and sell it to the highest bidder."

"Oh, Kingston, I'm not done, and neither are you. It's a few days before your birthday, so I was hoping you'd sort your life before then, but you haven't. So, here's your task. Go to the girl, or get the damn thing evaluated and never know love."

I shrug. "That's simple. The company is safe, so you have no hold. You won't do that to the others and we know it. Besides, that's something you can never know."

"This task is private for you, Kingston. You'll know. And you promise me if you go to her, you don't ever have it evaluated. You don't sell it."

I know what she's asking. It's trust and the one thing I hold close. My word. I could lie, but...I see what she's saying. But she doesn't get it yet. Sadie doesn't want me. She let me go. Hell, we weren't at a point where we had something. And me? Love isn't a thing. My mother just proved it's all transactional.

So, I give her what I want.

"Fine."

"Kingston—"

"It's real easy, Mother. I've chosen."

She stares at me.

"Evaluation. Love doesn't exist." I know this, because as I say it, love can't. And Sadie? She took my heart, stole it, and destroyed it. I saw her eyes when she said she used me. She meant it.

And even if it all is real, I can't trust that kind of thing. There's one thing I can trust. Money. "I'm getting it valued. It's solid and real and money doesn't lie."

"Then you lose everything," my mother says.

"Fine, Now go away."

And she does.

After she's gone, I pick up the tiara, turning it in my hands. Yes. It's better this way.

I don't need Sadie.

I don't need anything more than what I have.

At all.

# Chapter Thirty

## SADIE

It's been three days since everything imploded in my life.

Three days isn't enough time to heal a heart. Three weeks? Months? Years? Decades?

I don't know. I've never in my life felt this.

I look horrible. My eyes are red from crying and my throat hurts.

My father has been arrested and is on his way back to where he belongs. Jail isn't teaching him any lessons, and the irony of the new sentence he faces is due to trying to blackmail someone who wouldn't miss the thirty million dollars he tried to get.

He'll land on his feet in there as usual, no doubt. But it isn't my problem.

Three days and not one single word from Kingston.

I'm not proud of myself, but I've scoured print papers and online but he's not really mentioned.

Yia-yia said go to him, but I hung up on her because...what am I meant to do?

I destroyed myself and whatever tiny nugget of something I might have with Kingston to save him.

I know what he's like. And regardless of anything, even if this hadn't happened, we would never work.

"You need to get out of here," I mutter, and grab my coat. I fling open my door and freeze.

Kingston stands there, hand raised, looking like a thunderstorm personified.

He's so beautiful I could cry again.

I scowl. "Why are you here?"

He pushes past me without an invite and pushes the door shut, then glares at me. His eyes narrow. "You've been crying."

"Allergies."

I hate him. I can't even believe I cried over this man.

He slides a finger beneath my chin and his touch sends a shockwave of need and warmth through me. "It's almost winter, not spring. Have you been crying over me?"

His soft voice and gentle touch almost undo me.

"No."

"You know, you could say happy birthday."

"That's tomorrow."

"Oh look, she knows." He brushes my cheek with one thumb. The anger and annoyance is dark fire in his eyes and at odds with the loving touch.

I swat his hand away and step away. He follows. "Happy birthday. Now I've fed your pathetic ego, leave."

"I would if I could. But you..." He points at me. "You. You won't leave me the fuck alone."

"Me?" I laugh. "I haven't done a thing. I haven't contacted you at all. Some might say I've actually left you the fuck alone."

"Yeah. Exactly. It's annoying." He leans in close and drops his voice. "And you're still gorgeous when you've been crying."

"Do you even know how misogynistic that is? Why don't you just tell me I'd be pretty if I smiled and get it over and done with. Maybe give me an apron."

"And have you strangle me with it? No."

We glare at each other. It's like something savage needs to come out. And I feel suddenly, gloriously alive. "A girl can dream."

"You know, Sadie, I got the tiara."

"You're welcome."

He shoves a hand through his hair. "I was on my way to get the fucking thing evaluated, but I find myself here, instead. I even had a buyer."

He says this like it's an accusation.

"So?" I give him a shove. Which is a mistake because he's hard and warm and now I want to touch him more. "I don't work for you anymore."

"Is jumping my bones working for me?"

"Fuck you."

"Invitation?"

"No." Yes. But I keep that to myself, because I don't want just sex with this man. I hate him, I love him, I want it all. Forever.

And I don't know why he's here.

"I found a buyer and I came here instead."

"Do you want a medal?"

He exhales noisily. "You're such a pain in my ass. I don't know why the fuck my mother thought I had to choose between never knowing the value and you, and knowing the value and selling it and no you."

My head starts to spin. His mother did what? Because I don't think the tiara is a Minchini. It might be worthless, it might be priceless, but if he doesn't then this is about the other worth, the intangible and— "Me?"

"You."

"You're smarter than that."

He laughs bitterly, "Not where you're concerned."

"I can't help it if you make stupid decisions."

"No, you're just the fucking cause, Sadie. And it's only been three days. Three days where I've talked myself into all sorts of knots. I've told myself I don't care. I've told myself I'm better off without you. I've told myself you meant what you said."

"And what about you?" My heart's beating fast and something inside starts to glow. "I thought you didn't want me."

"I think I showed I wanted you."

"You told me to leave."

"Your fucking father was in the other room. And you—you tromped all over me."

"I was trying to protect you from him."

Kingston shakes his head. "No, I was trying to protect you."

"This is not what happened," I snap.

"Yeah?" He comes up close. "That's what happened. You showed me I have a heart, and then you destroyed it. I'd say you're the worst."

I put my hand on his chest to shove him again, but somehow my fingers tangle in his sweater. "No, you destroyed mine."

"You know what, Sadie?" He slides a hand through my hair, his fingers against my scalp. "I love that you're ruthless and you did all this for the money, but it really pisses me off."

"You're one to talk. You're ruthless and cynical and love money more than anything." I give him a contemptuous look even if my blood is singing. "So, what? I like money, too. I wanted the money and it seemed a good idea to make double the amount."

"I call that shady ethics."

"Says the fucking billionaire."

"To the thief."

I rise on my toes and brush against him, pulling him to me and our mouths almost touch. "I gave the money back to your mother. I didn't even have to because she wasn't out to get you. And you hired me yourself."

"You admit it."

"I can't admit something you know."

"You can, Sadie," he says, mouth a whisper from mine, his breath warm and I sway into him.

"But I gave that money back, Kingston. Mr. Billionaire. And you know what really gets my goat, what pisses me the fuck off?"

"I'm sure," he says like silk, "you'll tell me."

"I gave that money back for you. I didn't like you, and I didn't plan on liking you, on wanting you. I didn't plan on you being you. And I hate the fact I fell in love with you!"

"Yeah? Well, how do you think I feel? I didn't plan on liking you, on you being you. I don't want or believe in love. So how do you think I fucking feel? I'm in love with you, too!"

Silence slams down and we stare at each other and I want to cry all over again. But not like before. Inside something big and sweet and wild builds.

The savageness is love, and I...I could close this gap. I could kiss him and fuck him and we'd what?

"So where does this leave us?" I ask quietly. "You said...the tiara...you'll never know what it's worth if you choose me."

He half smiles. "I could lie and do it and my mother would never know."

"We won't ever work, Kingston. You'll know if you do that, and so will I. And you'll resent me if you don't and..." I breathe in and watch him. "And we're too the same. If we love each other, this will get to us and—"

"I cancelled the evaluation on the way. And the buyer," he says. "And we *are* too the same."

"What are you saying, Kingston?"

He kisses me, then. And it's the sweetest thing ever. Full of love and lust and latent passion, like we have all the time in the world. "You, I choose you."

"But the tiara—"

"I don't care. One of us needs to be pragmatic. Otherwise we'll fight ourselves into misery again and you'll come to me and we'll fight, we'll have sex and then we'll fight and you'll run and I'll come after you."

"You'll come after me?"

He nods. "It's exhausting. And I don't want to be back and forth. You admitted you loved me."

"And you said you loved me."

"So. Pragmatism. We work."

I kiss him again. "We fight."

"Yeah. We work."

"But," I say quietly, "you'll come to realize you want the tiara evaluated."

He lets go of my hair and slides his hand down my spine, pulling me in against him, and we fit. Oh, do we fit.

"I know the value."

"You do?"

He nods. "Yeah. You can't put monetary value on the priceless. And it's that, because of you. I know it's worth everything with you by my side. Even if it was made of string. And, without you?" He shrugs. "Worthless."

"By your side, huh?"

"Someone needs to keep you in line."

"You think you can keep me in line, Kingston?"

He laughs and it's so genuine it lifts my heart. "Actually, no. I don't think anyone can. I'm just offering you me. No thrills. Only me. And money."

"This isn't a transaction."

"I know—"

"Because real love isn't," I say, letting go of his shirt and taking hold of his face. He needs a shave. "I don't want money, or thrills like you're thinking. They're overrated. You're all the thrills I want. And I want you."

"I'm not good at this shit. Opening up, being vulnerable." He rests his forehead against mine.

"And you think I am? We can do it together. We have a lifetime."

He smiles. "Yeah. Yeah, we do."

Kingston captures my mouth in a kiss that's a promise and better than a ring. Because this is real if I want it. And I want it. I want him. Forever.

"Good," I say. "Because I want that. I want you."

"Then you have that. You have me. All of me. The good and the bad."

"I wouldn't have it any other way. You're going to drive me crazy."

He laughs again. "And you me. But we get to make up."

"I look forward to it." I take a breath and pull back. And I meet his gaze. "So...want to marry a reformed thief?"

"Yes. If you want to marry a ruthless, cynical billionaire."

"I wouldn't have you any other way."

And as we kiss again, it's a promise of the future. And I know this is right. This is good. This is love.

This is forever.

Me and Kingston.

For the rest of our lives.

*This is the end of Kingstion and Sadie's love story.*

*If you want to enjoy all of the Sinclair brothers (again,) and this time see behind the scenes of Mother Faye, start with Hudson's story "Dark Inheritance" or checkout my other books on amazon.*

# Afterword

Dear reader,

I really hope you enjoyed this story. If so, I would appreciate a short review on Amazon. As an indie author, I don't have the resources of a major publisher, so this is the way you would support me the most.

\*\*\*

A little note at the end

You will look for contraceptives in vain in this book. Why is that? The story takes place in your imagination and should give you a carefree time and carefree reading pleasure.

In this world, all billionaires have six-packs and are really good in bed. STDs don't exist in this world.

\*\*\*

Sign up for my newsletter and get my free enemies-to-lovers-romance instantly into your inbox:

https://www.subscribepage.com/rebecca-baker-english

Printed in Dunstable, United Kingdom